DATE			

REDHANDED

ALSO BY MICHAEL CADNUM

Calling Home

Breaking the Fall

Taking It

Zero at the Bone

Edge

Heat

Rundown

The Book of the Lion

REDHANDED

Michael Cadnum

VIKING

VIKING
Published by the Penguin Group
Penguin Putnam Books for Young Readers,
345 Hudson Street, New York, New York 10014, U.S.A.
Penguin Books Ltd, 27 Wrights Lane, London W8 5TZ, England
Penguin Books Australia Ltd, Ringwood, Victoria, Australia
Penguin Books Canada Ltd, 10 Alcorn Avenue, Toronto, Ontario, Canada M4V 3B2
Penguin Books (N.Z.) Ltd, 182-190 Wairau Road, Auckland 10, New Zealand

Penguin Books Ltd, Registered Offices: Harmondsworth, Middlesex, England

Published in 2000 by Viking,
a division of Penguin Putnam Books for Young Readers.

1 3 5 7 9 10 8 6 4 2

LIBRARY OF CONGRESS CATALOGING-IN-PUBLICATION DATA
Cadnum, Michael.
Redhanded / Michael Cadnum.
p. cm.
Summary: Since he cannot depend on his father, Stephen feels as though his only chance to make it to the big boxing tournament is to go along with the dangerous plan of a local tough guy to whom he has been introduced by a thrill-seeking friend.
ISBN 0-670-88775-7
[1. Boxing—Fiction. 2. Juvenile delinquency—Fiction.
3. Fathers and sons—Fiction.] I. Title.
PZ7.C11724 Re 2000 [Fic]—dc21 99-087652

Printed in the U.S.A.
Set in Berkeley

for Sherina

brick tower field
laugh lake sky

CHAPTER ONE

From the beginning he was too fast for me.

I tried to hit Del Toro, trudging after him with an unsteady, dancing bear gait while he shuffled and shimmied all over the boxing ring, flicking out his red-leather fists now and then, like he was warming up all by himself and I wasn't even there.

Then he started to hurt me. He jabbed hard, but I slipped some of his left-handed lightning. Several times I jerked my head to one side, so I caught the power on my ear, but after about a minute of this he started to time my head bobs.

He faked a punch and paused as I ducked to my left. I met the glove with my face and saw a vicious flare of light.

I almost dropped my hands right then, turned to Coach Loquesto, and said, I can't do this.

I was breathing hard, with that used-up, sour feeling in my lungs that comes from tense fatigue. Del Toro jabbed and then hooked to the body with the same smooth series of movements, without having to back off and set his feet. His left glove pounded all of Coach Loquesto's box-by-the-book lessons out of my head.

I shot a look to my corner, Raymond watching the fight sideways, like he couldn't stand to see it straight on. I had spent hours sparring with Raymond in his dad's garage, and he was the friend who had encouraged me to spend the last half year on punches and footwork.

I tried a technique I had picked up after hours, listening to the veteran amateurs, the postal clerks and carpenters who liked to box for the same reason some guys like to drink. They traded stories, half joking, half serious, how to cheat. I stepped on my opponent's white, pristine boxing shoes. I planted my right foot on his left, and leaned hard. I could feel his foot bones flatten out under the sudden weight. I heaved my left glove into his ribs and plowed forward like a football lineman, catching him in the chin with my shoulder.

He gave a little grunt, a likable, animal noise, like a very large dog lying down full of weariness. He gunned a combination up into my mouth, two staccato uppercuts, and danced away—far away, his legs a blur. He gave himself a little tap with one glove, adjusting the compact Everlast headgear and also showing me how to hit him in the head.

It's easy, he was saying. He flicked himself again with the oversized sixteen-ounce glove, daring me to plant a punch right there in the middle of his forehead.

Raymond was leaning into the ring, both arms on the canvas. His hands lifted in a classic beseeching pose, *be careful.*

I was gulping air, not even remotely in physical shape for this kind of workout. "I'm going to let you go three rounds with someone good," Loquesto had said, marking in my name with the squeaky black felt-tip he used, the Magic Marker ink smelling like rubbing alcohol.

I slogged after Del Toro, and he did a cute sashay to glide

way out of the reach of my glove. So I pumped my fist at him, not bothering to close my glove, trying to stick my thumb in his eye. He whipped a right cross at the side of my head. It landed, a punch I saw coming, and which my head rose to meet as though drawn to it by hypnotic suggestion. The blow momentarily paralyzed the right side of my face.

I continued to try to fight dirty, my body angled so Mr. Monday couldn't see what I was doing. Not because I disliked Lorenzo Del Toro, but because it seemed like all I could do, ashamed to be losing so badly. I dug my glove laces into his cheek, forcing them hard into his skin, and then when he recoiled, I trudged after him and gripped the ropes. I hung on with determination, using the ropes to pull myself toward him, into him, bearing against him with my whole body, ashamed that I had to fight like this.

By now the gym was going quiet, the echoing voices and the drumroll speed bag all falling still as people wandered over, aware that Del Toro was feeding me combinations, fast and mad.

Not out-of-control angry, but cold-pissed, his right hand cocked and ready to finish me while he painted me with his left. My mouthpiece got that raw-steak flavor you get when you're bleeding from the lips.

When the timekeeper called out, "Thirty seconds," I head-butted Del Toro in a style that belonged in a book of its own, a classic illegal maneuver, head down, bulling into his chest, and then up with a snap.

Even cushioned with the headpiece, the blow hurt me, the

point of his jaw outlined in the nerves of my scalp. I knew it did him harm. I then threw a classic cheat, one that it's impossible for a referee to fault you on, even when he sees it happen.

I feinted with my left just to set the foul up properly and make it look like an honest bit of boxing strategy, and I put all my strength into a straight right.

The straight right is a dream punch, one you rarely get to land because most opponents see you set it up. You get your feet just the way you want them, and stride into the punch, driving your gloved knuckles through your opponent's guard.

But in this case, I never really intended to hit him with the glove.

My punch missed on purpose, went straight by him. My elbow slammed into his nose, and I felt the gristle buckle. Guys watching called out a half-admiring, half-protesting, "Oh, man!" The *man* stretched out, the single word taking on the meaning: did you see that?

Del Toro put the heel of his glove on my face in the clinch—a little dirty combat of his own—and Mr. Monday, assistant coach and referee, was suddenly a presence in our fight, like a man who had just arrived. He pulled us apart, his hands slipping off our sweaty arms as the timekeeper rang the bell.

I wanted to enjoy this moment.

The round was over and I could stay as I was, expending no effort, except to disguise my weariness. I even gave that little wave that means *this guy is nothing,* a gesture wasted on Del Toro, whose back was turned.

I waddled, heavy and stiff-legged from the exertion, and

leaned against the ropes in my corner while Raymond squirted water on my mouthpiece, washing off the pink glue all over it.

"Well, you're still alive," said Raymond.

The small crowd around the ring parted as Loquesto made his way up to the ring apron, some of the spectators, with white towels on their shoulders or baseball caps on backward, acting out my head butt, my elbow punch, all of them eager to see if Loquesto would keep the fight from continuing, disqualifying me for fighting dirty.

CHAPTER TWO

This practice bout was scheduled to go two more rounds, but you could see Mr. Monday stroll over to the ropes, awaiting instructions from Loquesto to tell me to go take a shower.

Loquesto came over to me in his black sweater and his black, sharp-creased pants, looked over Raymond's shoulder right into my eyes and asked, "Holding up okay, Steven?"

"Great," I said, all I could manage, I was breathing so hard. I didn't want to meet his eyes.

He shouldered Raymond to one side and took my headpiece in his hands, forcing me eye to eye. "You're better than this," he said.

I shrugged one shoulder.

"If you don't show some class, you'll never make it to San Diego."

The Golden Gloves West Coast tournament was a month away, at the San Diego fairgrounds. If I could muscle up my boxing skills and get the registration fees and traveling money together, I had a chance at something big.

I let my gaze slide off his. But I gave a nod.

Loquesto sauntered across the canvas, and you could see him engaging in a silent laugh with Del Toro and his handlers, two older brothers with experience in the Junior Olympics, muscular middleweights. Loquesto gave a nod to Mr. Monday, a gray-haired, ebony-skinned man who always looked like he was listening to a ball game in his head, a playoff, his team way ahead.

Raymond is a short, thin guy, not quick enough on his feet to be much of a boxer. Raymond is the sort of person who might talk the two of us into climbing into the grizzly bear habitat at the zoo, and then cringe at the edge of the lair in real horror. He has a crave/disgust relationship with risk.

The rest period between rounds is always over before you know it. Andy, the timekeeper, hit the brass bell with the little wooden hammer that had been used for that very purpose since they began boxing in Franklin Gym sixty years ago. I rose to my feet off the wooden stool feeling that some mistake had been made—a minute could not have passed so quickly.

Maybe Del Toro wanted to buy a few seconds, too. He did that funny little hitch some boxers do, pulling up his boxing trunks even though with your hands wrapped and encased in padding you can't get much of a grip. His trunks still sagged a little, his pads exposed, bright pink kidney guards peeking out.

Mr. Monday called time-out. Del Toro glanced down, hitched at his belt, stopped and wrestled with his shiny blue trunks. Mr. Monday shook his head and stepped in front of him, grabbed his trunks, and gave them a tug upward, a valet adjusting a gentleman's suit. The crowd was patient, a couple of hand claps.

The entire gym wanted to know what would happen next.

So did I, and I didn't necessarily like the feeling.

Del Toro was adjusting his mouthpiece, giving himself a preparatory tap on the headpiece, the guy suddenly a mess of nervous tics. I walked across the ring. I dangled my arms, shrugged my shoulders, worked my head from side to side. Everything that happens in the ring is a contest, and I was intent on winning this beauty pageant, which of us looked most at ease.

Del Toro circled and was saying something around his mouthpiece, scuffing the flat, treadless surface of his boxing shoes on some water droplets Raymond had left on the canvas in front of my corner.

Mr. Monday observed this, and he called time-out again while Raymond leaped into the ring and wiped the canvas with a Bay Linen Supply towel.

The next few mental snapshots passed too quickly.

Raymond took a month blotting up the water, powder-puffing the dark patches on the canvas with a resin bag. He looked up and smiled hopefully, letting me know he was stalling, giving me a few more seconds of respite.

"Excellent job, Raymond," said Mr. Monday. He used to be a PE teacher at Merritt College, and even in semi-retirement you'd see him showing people how to fold towels, or set up a row of folding chairs, with a habitually encouraging air.

Del Toro threw a combination, far away from me, a practice one-two.

The next instant he hit me hard, I don't know with what hand.

Or how he leaped from several paces away, an opponent exactly my weight, but built like a real boxer, with a torso that looked too heavy with muscle to match those thin, deft legs.

I was hit. I understood that much.

And then, as I reviewed what had just been happening, I tried to convince myself that I had slipped on some of Raymond's water. I thought hard. I had been hit with a right cross, it was the only logical explanation. I was down.

On the canvas, my legs folded, like I was waiting to roast marshmallows.

I assembled myself, bone by bone, and when I was on my feet I became aware of Mr. Monday's count. "Seven," he said, holding out several fingers. "Eight," he said, methodically, looking over toward Loquesto, ready to stop it.

I jumped up and down, and said something, "I'm okay" coming out like caveman language around the mouthpiece.

"Suck it up, Beech," said one of the older men, a man in his thirties who used the gym as a workout establishment. "Hit him in the face, Steve," said one of the fourteen-year-olds. Nobody who knows me calls me *Steve.*

But I absorbed the sound of this, people cheering for me. I liked it. Del Toro ran a glove over the top of his head, dug a left hook to my ribs, and another one, punches that shook me. We clinched. I hung on hard, climbed into him, pinning his arms, bulling him back toward the ropes.

I landed a couple of rapid-fire combo, lefts and rights. You could hear the crowd suck air in surprise and pleasure. It looks pretty, when you do it right.

We wrestled, Del Toro needing a recess. I felt Mr. Monday's

shadow over me, and heard his breath, his teeth gritting together as he forced an arm between us, like a man reaching into the back shelf of a closet.

Mr. Monday said, like a man very mildly irritated with two little children, "I told you to break."

I hadn't heard him, and neither had Del Toro. Del Toro offered an apology with his eyes, his brows uplifted, and I held out a hand in a half-wave, both of us suddenly the picture of boxing manners.

Mr. Monday gave a signal, bringing invisible cymbals together, flat-handed: keep going.

But Del Toro and I circled, breathing deeply, buying a few seconds before we dived in.

CHAPTER THREE

"Good rounds," said Del Toro.

It was a hundred years later, and it was over, all three rounds of it. I let the mouthpiece fall out of my mouth, followed by a long splash of drool.

"Great rounds," I agreed, sounding like a talking dog.

Del Toro gave me a gentle, crablike embrace, his gloves impeding us as we hugged around the middle of our bodies, and slung an arm over each other's shoulders, as though someone was going to take our picture. He was panting, bleeding a little from his nose, but his respiration was already starting to level off. I felt dizzy, my breath sawing in and out of my body.

No one had a camera, and the crowd was already turning away, clapping with the perfunctory, cheery politeness of people with other things to do, the fight over, life losing much of its gloss. A few of them looking back to say something in Spanish to Del Toro, giving me a thumbs-up.

Coach Loquesto nodded at me, several silent up-and-downs of his head, like he was agreeing with a point I was making. I wasn't saying anything. I sidled my way through the entourage of a flyweight twenty-seven-year-old and his friends waiting to take their turn.

I felt great.

* * *

I showered and used some of the Alfred Dunhill aftershave Raymond had stolen from a department store—or so he claimed—twenty dollars an ounce unless you have smart hands. I laced on my street shoes, my hands feeling puffy and clumsy, while Raymond took random blows at the lockers with a knotted towel. When he struck a locker too loudly he flinched, and gave the metal surface a gentle swipe.

Raymond was saying that I could have killed Del Toro, if we met in the street. I let him talk for a while, Raymond tough now that it was over. Raymond was always yelling encouragement at his favorite team on TV, and then covering his eyes, afraid to look. We both felt excited by the fact I had survived three rounds with a fighter who had fought on amateur cards in Richmond and Modesto.

"I guess Chad couldn't make it," said Raymond.

"Better things to do," I said.

Chad was someone new in recent weeks, someone Raymond had bragged about, his new friend, the guy who'd been in jail. With an older brother in prison on a felony murder charge, Chad sounded like trouble. Raymond said Chad bragged about shooting a homeless guy down by Fruitvale Avenue, emptying a clip into him, but I didn't believe it.

"Chad missed a good fight," said Raymond.

Raymond's enthusiasm for things tended to win me over. He had introduced me to Loquesto, saying that the former light heavyweight was supposed to be a living legend, a real boxing expert, and now he wanted to introduce me to a new friend who was a criminal.

I could wait.

But I was teased by curiosity, and maybe a little jealousy. Chad and Raymond had been seen hanging around the Subway Sandwich place on MacArthur, fellow boxers reporting to me that Raymond's new friend was big. That's all anyone would say: "He's a big guy," like there was something else no one could bring themselves to tell me, how much trouble he might turn out to be.

The locker room had a fresh-paint smell, the metal lockers and the high, gleaming walls a fresh lake-water blue. The rooms were ancient, and had been painted so many times the pipes were layered with semigloss, painted fast to the walls. Our twenty-five-dollar registration fee rented us a locker; everything else cost extra. Not much money went into making the place pretty. If you got good enough to box in any of the regional or national competitions, it could run into hundreds of dollars in bus fare and hotel bills.

Raymond held the door for me, kidding, giving me a butler's after-you bow.

On the way down the hall Loquesto was Magic-Marking my name next to Stacy Martell, a security guard who'd been in the navy.

"You've got to be kidding," I said.

Stacy Martell was a natural middleweight with years of experience. He wouldn't be fighting as a novice except that he had two kids and never got in enough practice rounds to fully develop his ability. Our three-round bout was scheduled for Friday, five days from now.

"He'll murder me," I said.

I hate the noise Magic Marker makes the same way some people hate fingernails on a chalkboard. Loquesto was deliberate, wiping a little smear after my last name.

"You're ready for Stacy," said Raymond, stepping close to my elbow. "You'll mess him up."

Then he turned to the boxing coach. "Maybe five days away is too soon. Maybe a week or ten days is more realistic."

Loquesto gave a wise smile, as though mortal humans like Raymond and me couldn't understand the nuances of scheduling bouts. He put the cap on his marker, really forced it on, so whatever happened the ink would not dry. Loquesto used to joke around with Raymond, called him Sting Ray and Sugar Ray and other wordplays off his name. But in recent weeks he had just given Raymond a straight-on, almost pitying stare and said things like "Be careful, Raymond," or "Watch your back, Raymond," maybe not liking the thoughtful sideways look Raymond had begun giving things.

"Look at Steven, he's still bleeding," said Raymond.

Loquesto stepped close, peeled down my lower lip, taking hold of my face like an adult checking to see what a toddler has in his mouth.

"Seepage," said Loquesto.

He could speak Spanish, and even some lilting Italian when one of the old-time contenders dropped by, men who had boxed out of North Beach in the days when there were boxing clubs. I had the feeling that Loquesto relished the Latin tongues and felt that English was a flat-footed language, full of stops and starts. Sometimes I thought that if I spoke Spanish, Loquesto would spend more time with me, explaining what it was like to have a manager and slip punches for a living.

Even so, Loquesto gave you his full attention when he wanted to. "It's not a cut," he said, reassuringly. "Suck on some ice."

The fear of cuts haunts boxers. In a boxing match the only medicine you're allowed is adrenaline salve, and a cut inside the mouth is impossible to treat. You see hard-muscled veterans in great shape, except they bleed from old cuts after one round.

Loquesto motioned with his head and Raymond took a hint, sauntering up the hall. Loquesto waited for him to vanish through the heavy metal doors, white sun too bright to look at for a second.

"You're this close, Steven," Loquesto said. "This close to being really good."

A scar over each eye made him look strangely effeminate—his eyebrows looked penciled on.

I gave my head a toss, accepting the compliment.

He added, "You could be Junior Olympics top of the line, or come out of San Diego with a name. I put you in against Del Toro, and I'm wondering, maybe I should have a hearse standing by, all Steven can do is fight dirty, Del Toro will give him a brain bruise."

"Nice of you to worry about me."

Loquesto smiled. He turns it off and on, but for an instant you see the real person inside him, liking you. "I never worried. I'm kidding you, Steven. You don't look bad today, you land some punches, you show some maturity." He counted these points off on his fingers, like I might lose track of them.

I knew what was coming.

"You also try to fight like a gangster, like you were mugging some guy down on Foothill Boulevard. You knew that stuff wouldn't work against Del Toro. I'm surprised you'd even try."

I hate to make excuses. I kept my mouth shut.

"If you get in trouble out there," he added, "the tournament is out of the question."

Trouble and *out there* were both code words. For all Loquesto's bluntness, he wouldn't come out and say what he meant in English sometimes. He meant: Don't get mixed up with the police.

San Diego might be out of the question anyway, I almost replied, unless I got my hands on some cash.

He shot a look down the corridor, where Raymond was sticking his head back in through the metal doors.

CHAPTER FOUR

On the way to Raymond's customized Volvo we saw Del Toro and some of his friends, young men and women who looked like Latin movie stars, cowboy boots on the guys, perky breasts and tight sweaters on the women.

Del Toro gave me a salute crossing the parking lot, one raised fist. His friends flashed smiles. They were speaking Spanish. I knew that if I spoke the language I would be able to share some of that cheer.

By tomorrow Del Toro and I wouldn't feel quite so warm toward each other, but we would still be glad to be in each other's company. Boxing changes the way you feel toward your opponent. You could see it in the way Loquesto greeted his weathered pals who used to go ten rounds with him in Bakersfield and Tijuana. They meant something to each other, even after years.

Benny Gilmartin, Raymond's dad, gave me a slap on the shoulder. Raymond said, "Take it easy, he's been giving boxing lessons. Getting hit in the mouth."

Benny pulled his hand back, his broad face crinkled with concern.

"I'm okay," I said, and I did a little shuffle and tuck, showing off just a little.

Benny pursed his lips sympathetically. He had boxed in the army, as a cruiser weight. He never talked about his experiences, except to say that he was glad he tried it, and glad he stopped.

"It feels better already," I said.

I always liked coming here. The Gilmartin family had a stucco house on Golf Links Road, a tiny front lawn, and a huge, rambling backyard.

Raymond reached into the freezer compartment of the fridge, and brought out a mass of ice cubes frozen into a large chunk. The frozen asteroid was stuck fast together, and Raymond had to scrabble in a bottom drawer for a hammer.

"Whoa," said Benny. "You want to break off some cubes or smash it all to snow?"

"I know what I'm doing," said Raymond.

A couple of blows, and enough chunks had broken off to fill a plastic Safeway bag. Raymond handed me the bag, heavy with fractured ice, and I held it tentatively to my mouth.

I liked everything about the Gilmartin family better than I liked my own. Raymond's older brothers were hefty, tanned men who drove flatbeds or operated jackhammers, grown guys with new wives. Adam and Jesse got into manly trouble, found themselves being arrested for throwing beer cans onto the freeway, got into fights at Raiders games, but even municipal court judges liked them, sentencing them to community service. My own dad is an aspiring pianist, always out of money, and he never drives over the speed limit.

"The coach told you to do that?" Benny asked.

"Loquesto told me to suck some ice," I said.

"So suck," said Benny. "Don't stand around with an ice bag all over your face."

Raymond filched a couple of beers behind his back, a quick move, his fingers making a quiet, aluminum whisper as he tucked the cans under his shirt. "Steven's developing a real punch," Raymond was saying.

"I'm glad to hear it," said Benny. "We need kids who develop something." This was perhaps a criticism of Raymond, who I thought might be a disappointment to Benny and Sharon, always home late, unable to hold down a summer job. Raymond was out of step with his family. When all the other Gilmartins laughed at a show on TV, some character falling down or walking into a door, Raymond would just shake his head.

Sharon Gilmartin, Raymond's mother, worked for a paper warehouse, doing inventories on a computer. If someone lost a shipment of manila folders she found out where it was.

It had been right there in the Gilmartin backyard, under the large date palm tree, that I had learned the boxing basics from Raymond and his dad.

"I'm going to move the goats in about an hour," said Benny. "You want to come along?"

When I first started to spend time with Raymond and his

family, moving the goats was a highlight for all of us. Benny ran a brush-clearing service, cleaning hillside lands of fire danger. He operated a herd of goats that ate poison oak, tumbleweeds, star thistles. We used to help herd the quick-footed creatures, clapping our hands.

I wanted to be outdoors today, but Raymond had already decided what he wanted to do. He was heading out toward the small yacht, a gray ark on a boat cradle among the ivy. He was hunching to one side to hide the cans of beer faintly clanking under the tails of his shirt.

"Maybe not today," I told Benny.

Our feet crackled on the peeling varnish on the wooden deck. A mast had never been set into place here on this unnamed yacht, but it was easy to imagine one. For a few moments Raymond and I were like we used to be.

"Drink up," said Raymond as we settled into the cabin of the vessel.

We were miles from water. Benny had laid the keel and hammered the planks long ago, with a plan to christen the boat and sail her out to sea some distant, sunny morning. The cabin was naked plywood, warped in the corners around the nail-heads. The shadowy interior had a pleasant, earthy smell, years of mice and rain.

I rarely liked the taste of beer, that flavor of soapsuds and day-old bread. I took one sip, and heard Loquesto's voice in my head, counting off on his fingers what we were not supposed to eat and drink.

"Your dad's not going to notice a couple of missing beers?" I was asking.

"Drink fast," he said.

I sat there, listening to the sparrows in the big date palm outside.

"Chad's streetwise," said Raymond at last. "He sees things the way they really are."

I gave a little twitch of my mouth, something I had picked up from Dad, who liked to communicate without interrupting the symphony he was listening to.

Raymond rolled his eyes, and laughed an *aw-come-on* laugh that made me see him the way he used to be, when all we were trying to do was climb into a junkyard for the thrill. Lately he had grown silent and serious, worried about something.

I didn't like the way the beer made me feel, even after two or three swallows. I put the can out of reach.

"Businesspeople have insurance," Raymond was saying. "If some cash gets stolen, they report it to the insurance company, and get their money back. There's no such thing as a victim anymore."

I gave an openhanded gesture: maybe, maybe not.

"Your dad doesn't hesitate," Raymond was saying. "He'll buy himself a big expensive musical instrument if he wants it. Like that new thing he's buying. Everybody takes care of themselves, Steven. They reach out and take. Don't you get tired of watching everybody else cruise by with whatever they want?"

I put my head back against the bulkhead and closed my eyes. I could hear it in Raymond's voice: he wanted to be sure, but he wasn't. Raymond had always been this way, like the time we went down to the salt marsh, throwing rocks at passing freight trains. Raymond squinched up his eyes so he couldn't see what he hit.

"You wash dishes for minimum wage," Raymond said.

I let him talk.

"How much do you think your boss takes home, after taxes?" he said.

I said that I had no idea.

Raymond said, "The thing to remember is—whatever plan we come up with, nobody gets hurt."

"You told me yourself," I said, "Chad's brother got convicted of murder. His partner killed a gas station cashier, right? If you're involved in a crime where someone gets killed, it's the felony murder law. You get life in prison, even if you didn't hurt anybody." I watched the news, and I knew my facts were right.

"Chad makes me a little nervous, too," said Raymond quietly, flaking off a paint blister with his finger.

He added, "That's why I want you to meet him."

CHAPTER FIVE

My dad and I rented a unit in a twelve-story condo, part of a complex of buildings off 580 in Oakland.

When I was a boy and my mother and my father first moved there, I marveled that sometimes I could see the animals at the Knowland Park Zoo, a giraffe sticking its head high over the distant acacias, a zebra grazing on a golden hillside. One morning, for some reason I could never guess, a lion appeared, resting beside a chain-link fence. Even now, with the trees grown over the view, some mornings I thought I could see the placid profile of a bison through the greenery.

The day after the Del Toro fight, I left work early so I could be there when it arrived, my dad's new piano. I hurried across the plaza, my hands feeling pink and new after manhandling dirty pots for four hours. The job was just hellish enough to be fun, and you got free meals, all the sliced turkey and gravy you could eat, plus day-old desserts. I could spend time with Danielle, and besides, I needed the money.

I was a little embarrassed about being late, knowing how my dad felt about the delivery, nervous about it.

The piano was already hanging off the side of the building.

I took my place on the tiny strip of manicured lawn and

gawked, just like the others in the small crowd, neighbors with miniature dogs.

Two heavyset men held the thing steady in the late afternoon light, gripping ropes. Another man peered over from the roof, operating a Big 4 Rents winch. The piano was muffled up in a gray quilt, shrouded; you couldn't see what it was, but you could guess. The winch whined.

"I sure don't like the looks of that," said Mr. Torrance, a tall, red-faced man, a retired accountant. He was always laughing with my dad about his tax bill or his insurance premium, examples of amusing errors in math. He and his wife smoked nonfilter cigarettes, lighting them with old-fashioned Ronson lighters. Twilight and dawn you could see them walking their teacup mutt, standing far away from human habitation, flicking ash into the gutter.

Mrs. Torrance was a white-haired woman who used to run a lab, doing blood tests for Alta Bates Hospital. She read the latest news about the periodic table, who had just discovered what new element. She helped me with my chemistry assignments when I couldn't remember the scientific laws and rules. I still didn't understand the subject, but dogged memorizing and Mrs. Torrance's encouragement helped me pass the exams, and now I heard Mrs. Torrance ask, "How are your cations and your anions, Steven?"

"All my ions are okay," I said.

She seemed to think this was very funny.

I worried about Mrs. Torrance. She has a slight trembling in her hands, and with her interest in atomic particles, it seemed to me she ought to wonder what was going on in her lungs. She took my arm, and held her cigarette out to one side. She and Mr. Torrance often had me up to their apartment to eat hand-packed ice cream from a gourmet dessert shop on Piedmont Avenue. We would watch videos on nuclear accelerators or baseball games, which were almost exactly the same subject, as far as I was concerned, and load up on butterfat.

"I grew up with a Steinway," she said.

"Oh really." I really wanted to be polite, but I was very concerned about my father's piano.

"I hated it."

This seemed very much unlike Mrs. Torrance. "You don't like music?" I asked.

"I hated the lessons," she said.

I knew how she felt, recalling my father's look of anguish when I splashed yet another chord on the little Casio keyboard.

The manager, Liz Compton, marched across the tidy, bright green lawn and stood with her arms crossed. She was angular and unpretty, but so full of energy she radiated a sort of sexiness, if you like nerves.

"The elevator stuck again," said Liz, "or I would have been here sooner."

"Is anyone trapped?" Mrs. Torrance asked.

"Not the last time I checked," said Liz. My father attracts women like Liz—almost as smart as my mother.

More men showing up on our balcony, holding their arms out to the piano several stories down, as though to encourage it.

"Six men and none of them know what they're doing," said Mr. Torrance, an unlit Pall Mall waggling in his lips.

"Tripping on their dicks," said Liz, the sort of thing my mother would say.

Mrs. Torrance drew hard on her cigarette, maybe a little offended at Liz's manner and wanting to put a little smoke between her and such talk.

I tried to offer the opinion that they looked strong enough for the job, and Mr. Torrance gave a rumbly smoker's chuckle, winking at Liz, maybe flirting in an antique fashion, right in front of his wife. "It's leverage that matters," he said.

My dad joined the piano movers up on the balcony, a hand to his mouth. He caught sight of me and waved, his hand out like a traffic cop, as though to caution me not to spread my wings and fly up to join them.

The winch made an unsettling, wasplike keen. Without comment, all of us moved away from the lawn, leaving the rope holders plenty of space.

"Your poor father," said Liz. "He really looked forward to this."

The piano was developing a definite hitch in its position, an unmistakable cant. The winch whined, hauling the piano higher, and then too high, the piano creeping upward beyond where my dad was, leaning forward.

We all shrank back even farther, all the way to the tennis court fence.

You couldn't see the mammoth piano slip, but you could see a tendency, like when you know a row of books is going to topple.

This Bechstein beauty my dad had his heart set on was about to do a breathtaking plunge, all the way to the empty place near a half dozen retired people. And I found myself curious as I backed away from ground zero. How far would the piano keys scatter?

The winch was suddenly silent, and the piano slipped down, inch by inch. This made it possible for my father to reach out, straining over the side of the balcony, and touch the brass tip of one leg. He touched it with the pads of his fingers, but this little barely existent nudge was enough to move the quilted piano around in the beginning of a slow countercircle.

Dad reached that point in his own center of gravity that if one of the piano men had not gripped him, half jokingly, half in desperate earnest, my father would have taken a header and lofted down all that distance to the place where the lawn sprinklers were just sputtering on.

The automatic timer sprayed spidery water all over the two piano men near us, who flinched a little and said formal, manly things, like "Goddamn it," "For Christ's sake," making a show of not getting very upset by the water.

I was sure the piano would fall.

CHAPTER SIX

For an instant I considered taking an elevator, but a small boy was hammering on the elevator doors, shouting.

Everywhere you looked an EXIT sign was blinking off and on, or a clothes dryer ate coins without turning on. It used to be nicer in this building, and I hoped that someday, maybe when Mom came back to us, we could afford to move.

My feet made loud echoing slaps all the way up.

Dad was there, opening the door, showing me to the space the piano would occupy, a space of bare carpet. Potted palms and easy chairs were lined up against the wall.

By then the piano was slowly lurching into the room, the strong men easing her through the wide open glass doors, the quilt folding back around one of the ropes, mahogany gleaming.

My dad hovered close by, biting a knuckle, and the men heaved it into place, grinning with the strain, and then with relief.

"Maybe a little bit this way," my dad said.

I stepped over to the piano and hefted it myself, feeling how lean I was, surrounded by these men in green denims and baggy Bay City Delivery T-shirts, filling out those shirts pretty well, too, paunchy but with deep chests. I put some leverage into it, and felt my effort shift the piano.

"Good," said one of the men, with an accent, German or Scandinavian, that made the word sound guttural, an approval of my assistance that came from his bones.

"Good work," he said.

The concert-scale piano was too big for this room—way too big. In recent years my dad had made do with Casio keyboards, and always had access to a Yamaha at the college. The piano men folded the packing quilts, called down to the rope holders, made notes on a clipboard, having Dad sign by the *X*.

My dad gave them each a tip, a crackle of currency. He was paying for the piano by cashing in a certificate of deposit, the last of his inheritance from his parents' estate. Our furniture was mostly rented from EZ Life Home Furnishings on Frontage Road.

Mom and he shared expenses, but she was always gone, finishing her Ph.D. in animal biology, writing her dissertation on the tule elk. They are large, slow-moving creatures, cows with antlers. The species had been almost extinct until a lingering herd was rescued and allowed to roam some acreage north of the Bay Area. I had visited Mom a few times in her trailer, computer software and scientific journals stacked all over.

Mom spends her time studying with Dr. Urquist, the celebrity zoologist, and Dad has his girlfriends, a new one every three months or so. Women like his upbeat chatter, his ability to tell a joke one moment and sit down and play a sonata the next—and not just hit all the notes, but render it with feeling. After several weeks, however, Dad's women tend to screen their calls, and drift away to new terrain.

There is no great emotional explosion. It's just that Dad has only one act, one opening episode of his one, personal TV series, a guy with a winning smile and a gift for music. Months pass and you never see much more than that. It's just more small talk and a chance to go see a jazz guitarist he just heard about.

Dad clips grocery coupons out of the Sunday paper, keeping them in alphabetic order in the top kitchen drawer, paper towels right after meat loaf mix. I hear Dad on the phone sometimes, sounding full of high-octane enthusiasm for one of his new friends. I know he has another side, a side he never shows, the side that makes serious promises. I lie awake at night sometimes playing the scenes in my mind, how it will be when Dad stops being Mr. Wonderful and Mom settles back with us.

"My God, I thought I would die," said Dad when we were alone.

We leaned on the piano. I could make out my hazy reflection in the finish.

I ran my hand along the wood, just for the touch, the thrill, and gave it a gentle rap with one knuckle. A note answered my thump, a deep, sea dark intonation. Above the keyboard was displayed *C. Bechstein,* in faded golden letters. Way over to the right glowed the names *Kohler & Chase.*

My dad had not looked so happy in months. He teaches music at Laney College, one course, on appreciating music, and the class has a waiting list three semesters ahead. He used to have a radio show on KDFC, midnight to dawn, "The Masters Revealed," and even when he got phased out by computerized programming, local symphonies asked him to give a short pre-performance chat. When Dad says Mozart wrote the world's finest merry-go-round music, even the Mozart fanatics chuckle.

A knock at the door, and like a hasty afterthought one of the men carried the piano bench in one hand. He set it into place, thanking Dad again, adding, "Enjoy," as though the piano was something at a restaurant, the chef's special of the day.

Dad sat and played a power chord, a full-volume glissando.

"How about that?" he said.

"Terrific."

"It's a seventy-year-old piano." He sighed. "I'll have her tuned." He played a few notes of Chopin, his fingers tentative, like someone testing hot water.

Dad knows very little about boxing, although he has a napkin from the Sands Hotel in Las Vegas autographed by Muhammad Ali. He keeps it in the bottom dresser drawer, sealed in plastic. When I asked him to sign the waiver months ago, and told him I liked sparring, he had sighed and shaken his head. "You've never heard of dementia pugilistica? It comes from getting hit."

But I had praised Loquesto, raved about the gym, and said it was giving me a shot at the Olympics.

This last word got Dad's full attention. He kept a list of places he had lectured, Stanford, UCLA, and saw life as the process of building a résumé. With Dad, his own list of solo performances was more important than a bank account. I could see him gazing at me with a quiet pride in recent weeks, probably thinking, "My son, the Olympic contender."

Dad tested out the piano, trying to find things wrong with it. But enjoying it, too, improvising chords with a gentle touch, as though he had to sneak up on contentment or it would slip away. I stayed in the kitchen playing with Henry, the yellow parakeet. I wondered what Chad, this guy I had never met, would make of the way we lived.

The three-year-old bird did all the perky pet bird tricks, nibbled my fingernail, said its one phrase over and over, "How you doing?" It was a tiny, muzzy imitation of my father.

Henry hopped along the wooden perch, a span about as big around as a pencil. Henry was like a pretend bird, too cute, too happy, chirping and sparring with the little mirror hung inside his cage, the one he was sure held a very real pineapple yellow parakeet.

Henry mock-fought with the Mirror Henry, and I recognized that this was one of the training routines I followed myself, shadowboxing in the gym mirror, feinting and faking my own reflection.

Except my own image wouldn't hurt me.

Stacy Martell would.

CHAPTER SEVEN

Mr. Gartner had already given us a good-natured caution.

He hurried through the place just as I was pretending I was going to skim a salad plate over to Danielle's outstretched hand. Mr. Gartner was a heavy man with a likable, worn face.

It was the next day, and I could not be serious, looking forward to seeing my mom. Mr. Gartner clapped his hands, a sound you could barely hear over the gush of the dishwater and distant orders being given behind the swinging door to the kitchen. You could make out what he was saying: "Cut it out!" the way he always did.

Danielle made a half nod of apology, a winning expression that had to earn forgiveness but tonight just got a hurried, friendly glance from Gartner as he marched out into the employee lounge, where the waitresses touched up their lipstick.

Yancy wrestled a gravy pot over toward the sink, and I helped him, the hot, half-congealed turkey gravy slopping into the sink. Danielle rushed over to help, even though she didn't look strong enough to wrangle kitchen equipment.

Danielle was lithe and dark-haired. We had met three months before, at a first aid class taught at a fire department substation in the Oakland Hills. Giving mouth-to-mouth to a stoical rubber dummy and learning the arterial pressure points on a diagram, we got to talking about her interest in being a health-care professional, like her mom. She had an application form for this kitchen job in her daypack. She said that she would earn spending money, something to pass the summer months, and I stopped by the cafeteria and filled out an application, too.

Danielle starred in 98 percent of my own mental erotic adventures. In real life, Danielle and I had enjoyed two actual dates: a visit to the Cinemax in San Francisco, a 3-D movie featuring moray eels and lionfish, and an evening of thrill rides at a carnival by Lake Merritt, amusements that spun us upside down and rocketed us, yelling, in wide circles. Danielle and I were good at having ordinary fun together, but I was wondering how to dig deeper. I didn't know how to begin.

Steaming gravy splashed our arms and our apron fronts, but the two of us made a show of not minding the pain. The dishwasher was a big tray built in a circle, like a carousel. You stacked the spray-gunned dishes in the rubberized trays, making sure the glasses and cups were upside down, just like loading the dishwasher at home, except that this washer held hundreds of dishes at once. A multitude of dirty plates trundled off as the wheel turned, into a dark, whooshing hurricane.

By the time the glistening dinnerware reappeared from the washer, it was pristine and very nearly dry. The dishes were hot, too, and whoever unloaded the green-and-white Syracuse china had to wear special thick gloves, and even then got sweaty from the heat radiating from the piping hot flatware.

The stainless steel kept the heat the longest, knives and forks too hot to bare-hand out of the crate. I helped Danielle with this chore, grabbing fistfuls of forks and putting them over in the trolley, where the busboys would come in and take what they needed for the setups, the places on the dining room tables out in the real world. Danielle had said I was the best athlete she had ever seen, after watching me skip rope for twenty minutes, and sometimes I liked to show off.

I flipped a cup up into the air and did a basket catch, like an outfielder, and made a mock microphone out of one of the Duralex water glasses. You couldn't really talk with all the gushing and rumbling noise, and all communication was yelled and accompanied with sign language—"I need a mop" or "Your cap's on crooked" shouted and acted out.

Most of the time we bent our backs to our work, looking foreign to each other in the plastic caps Mr. Gartner ordered us to wear, like green shower caps. They made us look like medical technicians, people laboring in a humid emergency room.

The kitchen beyond was a room of wartime noise and frenzy. Even at our worst moments, with huge gravy pots carried in blistering hot, and hundreds of dishes piling up laden with half-eaten veal steaks and Thousand Island dressing, our chamber of hell was not half as hectic as the kitchen.

Sometimes the soup and gravy pots were so hot the dishwater sizzled, and it was sweaty labor, swabbing out the crusted minestrone or country gravy, using a stick-sponge and all my strength to work free the gunk cooked fast to the bottom.

That afternoon I was manning the spray gun, a coiled chrome hose with a grip-handle that powered a blast of water. Towers of barely eaten dinners would pile up in the stainless steel sink-top, and I would hose the food into the large metal trough. At one end of the sloping bottom was a hole, a serene maw that took it all in, not struggling or sputtering like the In-Sink-Erator at home.

Food that half an hour before had probably looked fit for the cover of a magazine was now disgusting to behold, and even Yancy, a man who had worked as a mess mate in the Coast Guard and scrubbed pots for cafeterias up and down the West Coast, shook his head when he saw some of the food wrecks that people had created.

I was blasting ricotta cheese, boneless chicken breasts, and crinkle-cut beets with the water gun, and I had it down to a rhythm. Three short bursts with the gun, and I turned and handed the plate to Yancy, who had sure hands.

Danielle and I would drop a cup every few days, and despite the sturdiness of the china a handle would break off, or a water glass would bounce off the rubber-grid mat on the floor and show a crack. "Sorry!" Danielle would sing out.

"Breakage," Yancy would call, meaning: no big deal. Kitchen work has its own terminology. A spill was *spillage;* sea crabs that showed up dead from the wharf, too rotten to cook, were *wastage.*

Danielle caught my eye, pretending she was going to flip something invisible off a spoon. She gave the spoon the wrong sort of tension, bending it back. The stainless steel spoon came to life for an instant. The utensil spun through the air, bounced off the rim of the steel trough, and fell into the gobbling hole of the garbage disposal.

Yancy moved fast, in a fluid, seemingly unconcerned way, hit a red kill switch down by the floor, and put his hand into the grind hole.

The sudden ceasing of the mechanical roar made the noise of the dishwasher distinct, a wet, mechanical chugging, and for some reason when Danielle made her sorry-about-that smile I did the logical thing. I fired the water gun right at her.

This spurt of water didn't do Danielle any harm. We were both sashed up in our plastic-cloth aprons, chest to knee, although my apron was covered with bits of meatball and stir-fry rice.

Danielle said, "Stop it."

I fired the water gun again, one more time.

Just as Mr. Gartner came through the door.

CHAPTER EIGHT

Yancy bent to rearrange some soup spoons in their cubicle.

Gartner nodded, making sense of what he was seeing, and what he was not seeing. He stepped over to the trough and peered into the silent hole, exaggerating, almost making a joke of it, a caricature, the Patient Boss.

The dishwasher raised a thunderhead of steam, obliterating Mr. Gartner's voice, forcing him to shout. He wanted to see us when our shift was done.

Yancy gave me a smile I could not mistake, a silent farewell.

I gave him a stiff, unreal smile right back, as though I didn't care.

We were waiting outside his office. It was twilight, and now, two days after my bout with Del Toro, my ribs were aching. Boxing soreness is like that, surprising you long after the fight is over.

Danielle and I waited in the corridor.

"Steven, you make such a big deal out of everything," said Danielle.

"Gartner thinks he can treat us like this," I said.

"Steven, look at you, full of all that tension," she said, sounding a lot like her mother, a sweet-voiced, no-nonsense woman.

Mr. Gartner breezed down the hall.

He hefted a key ring, picked out a key, and ushered us into a room of folders and software tumbling all over his desk, squashed soda cans in a paper bag, ready for that yearly trip to the recycling bin. A Hansen's coffee calendar decorated a wall, the entire year with phone numbers and notations scribbled all over it.

"You two find a place to sit," he said, falling into a mock leather starship chair.

I perched on a yellow plastic chair. Danielle leaned against the calendar. We had taken off our aprons, and washed our faces and arms, but even after all this time some of the pink was still in Danielle's cheeks from the dishwasher heat.

Danielle spoke first. "We're sorry we fooled around, Mr. Gartner, and we won't let it happen again."

"I've worked in restaurant administration for decades," said Mr. Gartner, giving her a save-it wave of one hand. "I have fired almost no one, for the simple reason that when it isn't working out most people quit."

"You want Steven and me to tender our resignations, Mr. Gartner?" asked Danielle, polite but not puppy-dog nice. "Because if you do, I really think you should rethink the situation." Her mother ran a staff of nurses.

Mr. Gartner settled back in his chair. He rocked back and forth for a while, relaxed and quite happy to be where he was. "I have fired personnel for drinking on the job," he continued. "For showing up high on drugs. And one time we had one individual try to stab another individual with a fillet knife."

"How awful!" said Danielle, maybe realizing the situation was flowing, Mr. Gartner wanting to tell his life story.

Mr. Gartner ran a hand through his balding hair. "I do believe we settled for disability in that case, because the attacker turned out to be a Gulf War vet with three kids and antianxiety medication that didn't work very well."

Mr. Gartner kicked off his shoe, a brown loafer, and tugged at the toe of his black sock. Danielle wrinkled her nose at me.

Mr. Gartner saw this, and he shook his head just slightly. "I like working in the bowels of an inferno," said Mr. Gartner. "Like today. Today the pastry chef is out with stomach flu, and forty people off a bus from Reno stagger in, pick up trays, and head for the salad bar." He chuckled and shook his head.

"And it gets worse," he continued. "Chef gets a speck of cayenne under his contact lens, and a customer finds a dime in the canned peaches, and then when I make it through the kitchen on my way to take a leak, two of our employees are playing war games with the hydraulic sanitation equipment."

"We were wrong," said Danielle. "And we're sorry."

Mr. Gartner's face would have looked good on a Supreme Court justice. "My problem is I really do like all this," said Mr. Gartner. "If I was your age, and saw myself running an insane asylum for a living, I'd think: this man is crazy. But I love it."

He looked at Danielle steadily, and Danielle looked right back, fresh and alert, with a sweet air that was absolutely genuine.

There was a long silence.

Mr. Gartner turned to me.

"So what I'm going to suggest," he said after thinking for a while, "is that you two work different shifts."

"You hired the two of us together," I said. I hadn't spoken for so long that I hardly recognized my voice.

"I signed you on at the same time," said Mr. Gartner, "but not necessarily as a team."

"One of us goes, we both go," I said.

Mr. Gartner put on his shoes, easing his feet into them, tapping the heels against the tiled floor. "Steven, let me talk with you alone."

Danielle trailed me in the parking lot. The East Bay summer nights are often cold, and I wished I was wearing a jacket.

Interstate 580 rumbles past on the other side of the lot, trucks sighing by, going eighty miles an hour. I wondered what Raymond was doing right about then, probably hanging out with men who carried concealed weapons.

"You told him okay, you'd work nights," Danielle was suggesting hopefully.

I kept walking, keeping my mind focused.

I was way ahead of Danielle, and she had to raise her voice, calling after me. "Tell me you didn't quit."

CHAPTER NINE

We were driving down the freeway, toward Chad's house. I had called Raymond the night before, said I wanted to go visit his new friend, and Raymond had made the arrangements. Raymond gunned the open-air car out of the slow lane. It was a little past noon, and we were supposed to be there at twelve-thirty.

The next day I was set to fight Stacy Martell, and the entire gym was alive with the upcoming bout when I dropped by to pound the speed bag and shadowbox in front of the floor-length mirror. The Spanish-speaking guys said things I didn't understand, smiling and making punching motions. The older, experienced boxers wished me well, in a way that made me nervous and proud. "Don't mess him up too bad, Beech," one of them said, a thick-necked, coffee-colored welterweight with graying hair who, the story went, once fought a preliminary in Vegas.

I had worked in front of the mirror for hours, silver with sweat. Body hooks, head bobs. Getting that special, commanding look in my eye, like I could see through walls of steel. Andy, the timekeeper, said he'd heard that if I handled Martell, San Diego was a sure thing.

Raymond changed lanes and asked, "How are you feeling?"

I stretched my fingers to show that my fists weren't sore, which they sometimes can be, from working out with the thin speed-bag gloves. Dad took meticulous care of his own hands, wearing cashmere-lined gloves on even a slightly chilly morning, flexing his fingers unconsciously in idle moments, his hands nervously eager to be off and running. Years of keyboard lessons from Dad meant I could snap through Mozart's "Turkish March" without a note out of place, but Dad and I both knew I had about one-tenth his natural ability.

"I mean, about meeting Chad," said Raymond.

"Chad is no big deal to me," I lied.

Raymond let me see him thinking about this.

"Chad says Loquesto was a bleeder who couldn't go the distance after he turned pro, so he ended up picking up a little extra money."

Raymond was making sense, the sort you hate to hear. Loquesto was always smooth and well dressed, and liked to rivet you with his stare, a man pushing forty, an air of defeat about the way he probably dyed his hair.

"Okay," said Raymond, as though I had made some additional remark. He made a little down-turned shrug with his mouth. "If you're happy, I'm happy."

Even when he was accepting and forgiving, there was an alternate, opposite view, and he let you see it. "It's just, you can back out of this if you want to."

"I said I better meet Chad."

"But it doesn't have to be today."

"You ashamed of me, Raymond? You think Chad'll take one look at me and think, what's so tough about this guy?"

"We'll see Chad right this afternoon," Raymond was saying, "if you want to."

"That's what you agreed to."

Some part of me wanted never to have a conversation with Chad, the way some part of my body wanted never to drive one hundred miles an hour on the freeway ever again, hanging on the steering wheel like I had a few weeks before, Raymond in the passenger's seat asking why couldn't we go any faster, in a thin, scared voice.

Raymond said, "Chad tells me Loquesto used to throw fights for money, down in Mexico."

"You don't believe that," I said, knowing how much Raymond used to admire Loquesto.

"Not really. But I wonder."

That made me mad. I said that Chad was a liar. I actually used the word *liar,* realizing how biting and challenging it was.

Raymond drove along for a moment. "Do you think you'll be able to say that again? Explain to Chad how he's making up stories?"

I didn't bother making a sound.

"I can't hear you, Steven," he said.

"I'll tell Chad he's a liar," I said, aware that I was being cock-proud and foolish. "To his face."

"Really?" said Raymond, with a note of caution.

Or maybe it was the real thing, real glee. I couldn't read Raymond's moods so well anymore. He swung the car into the fast lane.

He said, "This is going to be fun," his voice cracking with tension.

CHAPTER TEN

Raymond and I rarely came into this neighborhood, the flatland district of San Leandro.

We cruised past storefront churches and insurance agencies, a neighborhood of overweight bikers, Harleys and Kawasakis sweating oil onto sidewalks. We passed flat-roofed blue and pink stucco building and blank windows, palmists and burglar alarm specialists.

Raymond drove a vintage Volvo his brothers had decided should be turned into a convertible. One fine, beery Saturday afternoon had seen Raymond's brothers laboring with hacksaws and acetylene torches, transforming this staid Scandinavian car. Now the gray two-door was open to the sky, with a long I beam welded across the backseat to give the vehicle strength.

Raymond pulled the car up a driveway and up onto the front lawn, parking under a spreading Monterey pine.

The front lawn was worn and rutted, areas of bare loam where cars had kept the sun from the grass, and a brown-and-black Doberman stood on his hind legs behind a chain-link fence and gave out a bark. Then he found a sag where the fence parted from the pole, stabbed his snout through the gap, and let out a low, bone-chilling growl.

The house was a tall white Victorian, handsome and genteel, except for the iron bars on the windows on the first floor and the flaking paint of the window frames. A blue wicker chair with a calico pillow sat on a broad front porch, overlooking the view of a taqueria and car stereo discount shop.

Raymond wiped his hands on the front of his pants and gave me one of his tight little smiles, his hand in no hurry to push the doorbell button.

Even in this broad afternoon sunshine a tiny electric light shined from within it, through the fingerprint grime. Raymond pushed the button, and as he twitched another smile at me I realized he had never visited Chad here at home before now.

And I felt some compassion for Raymond, unable to back out from the situation, with the whisper of the doorbell echoing in the interior of the house. I also realized something else as Raymond eyed me up and down, measuringly. Raymond was looking forward to showing me off, while I still had the nerve to call Chad a liar to his face.

Raymond was trying to find out something about Chad, and I was the test.

A pale young woman peered out through the screen while the Doberman at the side of the house barked full voice, leaping at the fence.

Raymond spoke, although I could not make out the words, a quiet politeness coming over him.

I barely heard her response: "My brother isn't here right now."

I was more aware than ever how I looked, my clothes whatever my dad and I had been able to pick up at the clearance table at Ross Clothes-for-Less.

"Carrie, this is great," Raymond was saying, "I'm very pleased to meet you at last. Chad is always saying wonderful things about you."

The young woman did not respond to this. She was not as pretty as Danielle, and did not have Danielle's winning smile, but I wished I had taken a moment to comb my hair.

"We're going to play tennis up at Hiller Highlands," Raymond added. "We hope to rent some rackets, work on our serves."

He might as well have said we were going to play nine holes of golf at Pebble Beach. Hiller Highlands was a development far up in the hills where freshly painted concrete courts were enjoyed by dentists' and podiatrists' wives.

But the young woman hesitated, conquered by Raymond's talk, maybe, or by my look of apology. Or maybe she was just afraid of Chad's anger, whatever her brother would do if she turned us away.

"We're a little early," I said.

She unlatched the screen door and let us in, the Doberman going crazy behind the fence.

"Who's this?" said a kid looking right at me, one of those tough junior high students who move with a swagger, even in his own living room.

"These are Chad's friends," said Carrie. She turned to us and asked if we wanted to sit down.

"Steven is a boxer," said Raymond, with something close to pride. He moved a sports section of the newspaper to one side and sat on the couch. I took my place in an old oak rocker, trying not to let it shift back and forth.

Raymond continued, "He's a welterweight, in the novice division. The coach thinks he can make it to the Junior Olympics or maybe even the real thing, Team USA."

"How big is welterweight?" said little brother.

"Steven goes about one-forty-seven," said Raymond.

"Not very big," said the kid.

"Just about right," said Raymond, putting out a playful hand, as though to cuff him gently all the way across the room. "Boxing fans don't usually like size. Big equals slow."

If I made it to open division boxing, where you fight opponents who have real ring experience, I hoped to muscle up to middleweight, or even light-heavy, without losing my speed.

"On Monday, Steven fought Lorenzo Del Toro, a nineteen-year-old man with a three-and-oh record," Raymond was saying, maybe too nervous to shut up. "Steven put a whole lot of pressure on him."

The dog outside continued to go insane.

CHAPTER ELEVEN

A large flowering plant branched from the dark fireplace, fake calla lilies. On the mantel was a picture of Jesus, looking away from us, toward a source of light that radiated from above.

In another framed picture a large young man with quiet gray eyes looked out at us, his arm around a tall blond kid with a basketball. Both of them were smiling, the sort of happiness you can't fake. "That's Milton and Chad, years ago," said Carrie.

"Chad's older brother," said Raymond. "He's in Vacaville, in the prison. He's always getting into fights in the exercise yard."

Carrie indicated a large three-ring album on a shelf. "There are more pictures in there," she said. "And letters Chad keeps, from Milton."

The Doberman's barking took on a hoarse, maniacal note. Or maybe he was getting tired. Little Brother slipped away.

Carrie watched Little Brother leave, and then took the album from the shelf. She turned the pages possessively, letting us see the contents without actually sharing them. I glimpsed handwriting on lined paper, black ballpoint pen. "Chad keeps every letter."

Carrie eased a snapshot from the album and handed me a view of Milton and Chad, unmistakably the same two people.

Milton wore a gray work shirt and matching gray pants while Chad had grown up, filled out, and gotten a set of muscles. But he kept his proud smile. The two brothers beamed at the camera, while behind them blurry picnic tables and chain-links offered a sample of what I took to be visitors' day at a correctional facility.

"Mom works as a dispatcher for Friendly Cab," Carrie said, maybe to explain her absence. "We rent the bottom floor; upstairs are the Websters. They sleep all the time." She was quiet for a moment, maybe feeling she didn't owe us even that much information. Maybe having a brother in prison, and another one as big and sure of himself as Chad appeared to be, made her want to talk. She closed the album, put it on the shelf, and said, "Would you like some apple juice?"

The dog was going completely crazy, somewhere under the house by the sound of it, and I felt the intrusion of our visit, Carrie going out of her way to be civil to the two of us.

When Little Brother came back into the room and said, "That cat got under the house," it was a welcome chance to leave the place, the walls gradually closing in.

Carrie showed us through the kitchen, a room with a high white ceiling and duct tape holding a pipe in place beside the water heater. Raymond stayed to one side of the back porch, over by a mop head dried stiff and gray. I took my time going down the steps, the Doberman peeling back the skin of his muzzle in a chilling display of white teeth.

I couldn't bear to look at the dog, even though Carrie said, "Bullet, go lie down," and the beast retreated a few paces back.

Little Brother and Carrie stayed on the back porch, and Raymond was halfway down the steps. The Doberman was growling and slavering at me as I stood there trying to stare him down. Now and then he would dodge over to an opening under the house, a space big enough for a large man to crawl into. Between the space under the house and me, he couldn't decide which drove him most crazy.

"If you get the dog calmed down, I'll rescue the cat," I said. "I can't do it with the dog about to eat my body."

I had the mental image of my rear end being torn to pieces, and I had the impression everyone else had the same thought. Plus, Chad would be home just in time to see paramedics putting my remains into a body bag.

Carrie made it all the way down to the bottom step, and she gave a soft, all but inaudible whistle, and confused the dog-monster just a little. She hooked a single finger under his collar and gave me a guarded smile, not with her mouth so much as with her eyes. It was a little challenging, daring me to get down on my hands and knees and crawl under the house.

"What color is this cat?" I asked, as though there might be a dozen animals under there.

"It's white and gray," said Carrie. "With black points on its ears."

I crept on my knees to the gap in the white wire screen that shielded the dark under the house, and bent the wire lace slightly, peeling it back. White flecks of paint came off on my fingers.

The gap was smaller than it looked, and under the house it was very quiet.

The dirt in the darkness was soft and rose up into the air, like sifted flour. Spans of spiderwebs caught the dimming sunlight overhead, and when I tried to rise up, my head hit the underside of the house. Dust-laced webs trembled overhead, and I breathed a taste of cold soil, decaying lumber, mildew.

I avoided a bent nail in the dirt, and a white porcelain knob. A broken half of a blue-and-pink tea saucer impeded me briefly, until I set it aside in the bad light. Nobody had to rescue a cat from a refuge like this.

But pride kept me there, calling, "Kitty, kitty," flat on my belly in the grime.

Eyes glittered. Reproachful, round eyes, and when I called in my gentlest voice, the eyes gazed steadily right at me, unwavering.

Raymond's voice reached me as though from an unearthly distance, asking was I all right.

I was far from daylight now, hoisting my body forward. Black widows loved dark, neglected places like this. The space was shrinking, the floorboards above pressing down on my back, my shirt catching on splinters in the wood.

The floorboards overhead creaked.

A heavy, deliberate tread crossed the room just above, and the steps continued, in no hurry, until I could not hear them. Raymond fell silent. The dog was quiet, too.

The cat was a dim shape, hunching, retreating from my hand.

I stretched my fingers, and the cat gave a low, disturbing sound, a throaty grumble.

I did not flinch, my hand extended.

I touched soft cat hair, stroked it with the very tips of my fingers.

Back in daylight the air was warm, the sun heavy and scented with honeysuckle.

The snapshots had not prepared me for Chad.

CHAPTER TWELVE

He was tall, but not giant, only six one or so, built like a heavyweight, with broad shoulders. He was in solid shape, no tummy fat at his belt. He hair was yellow, like fake coloring, bright blond. It was his eyes that stopped me right where I was. Blue-gray, with a steady gaze, he looked at me like he could see into my mind.

I looked right back. It's the first thing you learn as a boxer, the prefight stare. But fighters are half bluff, trying to fake each other out. Chad was actually using his eyes to observe me, measuring, about to pass judgment. Something about his gaze, and the possibly pleasant, possibly menacing openness of his expression made me want to win his favor.

Raymond kept off to one side, his arms folded.

Chad extended his hand, and I shook it. Dad once told me you want to shake hands not too hard, not too soft. Chad's handshake was all grip. I squeezed right back, and his eyes crinkled. He released my hand, and we both grinned, as though some point had been made.

"You hurt yourself," he said.

I studied my hand. The cat gouges began as shallow rips, and then welled with blood where the claws had found meat. The blood was already drying, dark pearls. It was nothing that would keep me from fighting, although Loquesto would tell me I should take care of my fists.

"Cat," I said.

"Not that old sick black-and-gray cat that couldn't hurt a baby?" asked Chad, in a softly teasing tone.

"Bullet chased it," said Little Brother, watching all this with interest.

"That old wasted cat that has cancer?" Chad asked, just a little more playful sting in his voice.

"Chad, you are a disgrace," said Carrie, with no attempt to lighten her words. "I'm going inside to get some medicine," she said.

"That's the world's feeblest, oldest feline," said Chad, with a little lift of his chin.

Raymond stayed quiet. I didn't know if I should rise to the insult, or laugh.

"Besides, didn't the police come around here last week saying look out for a cat with rabies?" said Chad. He stretched out the word, so it sounded like a strange name for a grotesque disease: *ray-bees.*

This was where Raymond had picked up his recent diction, a jailhouse, faintly Texan lilt. Raymond was full of convict lore lately, things he'd learned from Chad. Raymond maintained that men who have done time don't walk like the rest of us but adopt a habitual, loose-limbed, self-protective stroll, a pace not intended to cover ground.

For some reason another smile forced itself across my face.

Chad was funny, in a flat, edgy way. This was a surprise. Little Brother swallowed a sigh, none of this as entertaining as he'd hoped. He picked up a little twig and broke it, swinging the broken twig bit around in the air, hanging by a thread of bark.

"Steven wanted to talk to you about boxing," said Raymond.

Chad would be a tough opponent, taller and heavier than I was. Maybe a lot heavier. Chad gave the impression of powerful, jaded adulthood. Raymond had said he had just celebrated his nineteenth birthday, eating well-done sirloin and every single cherry tomato at the Sizzler's all-you-can-eat salad bar.

The metal trowel stuck into a patch of geraniums, the brass nozzle of a garden hose—I tried to size up the space we were in, what I could hurt Chad with if he stopped teasing and got suddenly cold eyed. Because that could happen, and Chad let me see it in his expression. You wanted Chad on your side in a fight.

Raymond said, "We were talking about Loquesto."

Chad closed his eyes and slowly opened them, as though the boxing coach's name was beneath mention.

I lifted my shoulders, high, all the way up to my ears, and let them fall, the quickest way to loosen your arms when you don't have time to warm up.

Carrie made no sound as she made her way down the back steps holding a small white tube in her fingers. She hesitated, and waited until Chad motioned, go right ahead.

I didn't want to acknowledge the claw marks just now, and yet something about Carrie made me accept the white tube. I squeezed some white ooze over my scratches, and rubbed it in.

"She's my only sister," said Chad.

As he said this he shifted his head from side to side, maybe demonstrating how he'd avoid a punch if anyone tried to hit him. "I try to make sure no puppy dog comes sniffing around the wrong bush," he said.

Joking, not joking. Chad gave a nod and Carrie and Little Brother vanished up the back stairs. I could see why my boxing friends had described him as *big*. He owned the space he was in.

"I have been trying to think of a couple ways I can help you two get your hands on some spending money," he said. "Because I'm a kind person, and I take an interest in my friends."

He dug into his pants and brought out a roll of currency with a bright red rubber band around it.

The rubber band made a high-pitched sound as he eased it gently off the roll. The money opened up in his hand, straightening partway, bent like a horseshoe.

"Buy yourselves some clean clothes," said Chad.

I made no move to take the bills he was holding.

"I owe it to you," said Chad.

A slight wind ruffled the money he was extending to me, the breeze fluttering the gray-green paper. I could see that under a couple of fifties and twenties, the cash was all singles.

"For getting all dirty, helping my sister," said Chad.

Raymond turned away, strolling over to a Colonel Sanders

carton squashed beside the garbage can. Raymond made a show of tucking the trash into the can as Chad put the roll of currency back into his pocket, unaware that I had seen how little money it really was.

The insight made me feel strangely protective of Chad, as though I knew he was half bluff.Chad smoothed out the marks I had left in the dirt by the opening under the house, scraping soil over the specks of white paint. "Raymond, what do you know about Pontiacs?"

"The cars?"

"Pontiac cars, that's right."

Raymond looked my way, his eyes uncertain. "My brothers and my dad have better luck with foreign cars."

"Like your beautiful special convertible Volvo," said Chad.

Raymond laughed.

"A man just offered me a Pontiac outside Pic-n-Pac Liquor," said Chad, in a tone that let us know he was having some fun with us. "I think I made a mistake. I paid him cash and drove it away."

We followed Chad through a side gate, out into the front yard, where an Arctic white Firebird rested under the pine tree, making quiet, inward sounds as the engine cooled.

"It's got a V-six engine, standard," I said. "Two hundred horsepower at five thousand two hundred rpms. If you don't move it, those birds are going to make droppings all over it."

"You have one of these?" asked Chad.

"I tried to get my dad to consider a new car," I said. One of my favorite classes at Hoover High was automotive engineering. Dad had said we could lease what we needed. What he thought he really required was this seventy-year-old grand piano that he had found advertised on a music store bulletin board.

"It's hard to drive this car," said Chad.

I peered through the passenger window. "It's got five-speed manual transmission," I said. "You probably drove down the street popping the clutch."

"Popping the clutch," echoed Chad, relishing the phrase.

"Let's go for a ride," said Raymond.

"I'm not getting into this car," I said. I had a clear mental image of police units, the three of us handcuffed and arrested for receiving stolen goods.

At the same time I could see the pull Chad had on Raymond, and I felt it, too. This tall man with yellow crayon hair knew a world I had seen only on TV, a landscape of handguns and street cops. I wanted him to like me.

"He's not going to sit down in my car," said Chad, in an explanatory tone walking over to Raymond and handing him a set of car keys.

Raymond shot me a warning look.

"Why not?" asked Chad. "Afraid it doesn't have seat belts? Afraid the brakes don't work?"

Sometimes you talk, sometimes you don't. I kept my mouth shut.

Chad smiled.

"Your friend is a smart man," he told Raymond.

I felt a flush of pleasure.

Smart man.

A shaggy brown dog, part sheltie, had been making his way stiffly along the sidewalk. The dog nosed the air, scenting the Doberman perhaps, and doubtfully eyeing Raymond and me.

Chad held out his hand and called to it. The old dog gimped all the way to him and licked the air hopefully.

Chad took a moment, talking to the dog in a quiet voice, caressing it gently.

Then he turned to the two of us and said, "Let's go."

CHAPTER THIRTEEN

Chad told Raymond to drive the Pontiac north on I-80.

The traffic was backed up close to the Bay Bridge, but Chad looked out at the lanes of slow traffic, nodding like someone who heard music in his head, sitting in the passenger side of the front seat.

When we passed a Highway Patrol unit that was stopped to help a stranded car, Chad watched the patrolman until he had to turn his head as we passed. Chad caught my eye and made a pistol with his fingers, and a series of soft, plosive reports in the direction of the highway cop.

We took an off ramp and drove along San Pablo Avenue. It was a sunny afternoon, and when Chad saw young women waiting for the light to change, hurrying along the crosswalk, he called them "jailbait" and "split tails."

I am always embarrassed or irritated by guys who talk trash about women, and I wondered why Chad felt he had to make such comments.

"You can't even trust a bitch to make it across the street," Chad said as a woman with a limp made us wait, slow to get out of the crosswalk as the light turned green.

I could sense Raymond trying to flash me a glance in the

rearview mirror, wanting to know what I was making of all this, half hopeful, half nervous. Raymond wanted me to say something, but I wasn't ready.

"My brother's wife is talking about divorcing him," said Chad. "Can't wait for him to get out of prison, has to cut and run."

I said that I was sorry to hear that, glad I had kept my mouth shut until now.

"She used to be okay," Chad said, in a tone of regret. "She told me all about stream fishing, fishing lures, fly casting. She knew all about trout."

I was about to ask if he liked to fish, just to ease the conversation away from a painful subject.

"Look at these storefronts," Chad said abruptly. "Check cashing places, liquor stores, asking for trouble. Begging for it, some reason to make their insurance pay off. They have low-surveillance security, and rent-a-cops too slow to work for the post office."

Maybe Chad could hear my unasked question.

"I can't scout these sites all by myself," he said. "And get my face recorded in the video. If word got back to my brother, he'd have me killed, just to teach me a lesson. We need someone fresh."

He looked back at me and winked. "Can't you smell that money?"

I gave a little half laugh, so both of them knew I thought Chad was just fooling around.

* * *

We stopped at Nation's Hamburgers on San Pablo, right across from a furniture store, big windows with leather sofas and pretty little coffee tables.

Chad insisted on sitting in a booth. "One over there, with a view of the parking lot," he told the woman at the counter.

The three of us waited until a booth was vacated by three very short, dark-haired men, one of them with a yellow Golden Gate Fields stable pass hanging from his belt.

"Jockeys," I said as we settled into the seats.

"Watch your mouth," said Chad. "How do you know those guys have jock itch?"

I began to explain that they were probably jockeys from the racetrack across the freeway, but then I saw Chad's grin. He picked up a slice of dill pickle left on the tabletop, and made a motion like he was going to skim it over to me.

I couldn't see this big-boned, good-humored guy using a gun on anyone.

When a police unit rolled into the parking lot, right past the white Pontiac, Chad stopped swirling the ice water around in his glass. The cops were coasting very slowly, and Chad leaned forward to watch as the two cops conferred in the front seat of their city of Richmond squad car.

Chad put both hands on the table, and I thought that he was ready to bolt out of the booth.

Then one of the cops came in to place an order to go, and Chad sat back. He started in on a story, how his brother gave him his first basketball, and how convicts play one-on-one in the prison yard.

* * *

Chad and Raymond dropped me off outside the Buccaneer Cafeteria, near the back entrance, where the offices are.

"You work here?" asked Chad. He squinted around at the building, the row of Dumpsters, the parked cars, his expression full of mock pity and amazement, *How can people live like this?*

They left me there, Chad giving me a wave out the window.

Marlo, the woman at the pay window, beamed at me, crinkling her eyes behind her half-lens glasses, but she said I couldn't have my final paycheck until "the end of the payment cycle," nearly two weeks off.

I wanted to make more of an argument, but I wasn't really surprised. "Could you look in the computer and see—maybe they could make an exception."

"Oh, Steven, the only time there's an exception is if you die. Mr. Gartner cuts a dead person's check right away."

Marlo is one of those people with rings on almost every finger, silver in various patterns. She fidgets with the rings as she talks, as though none of them are quite the right size.

"But a dead person wouldn't actually have much need of any money," I said. I had the feeling that Chad would have approved of my approach.

"That shows what you know," said Marlo.

"Make believe I'm dead," I offered.

"Plus, only three days into the pay cycle, with your laundry bill, which covers the cleaning of work apparel, the withholding taxes and the Social Security and the workman's comp payment and everything else, you might not want to count too heavily on the check."

"You could give me an estimate," I said.

She popped the end candy off a tube of peppermints, a round pill she put on the end of her tongue.

I delayed leaving, timing my visit to see Danielle come off duty, and when she did she was walking with Hugo, a line chef from the kitchen, a tall, red-haired guy who spent a lot of time with tiny earphones, getting them to fit into his ears just right. Even now he had earphones around his neck, the thin, stringy kind, like a fashion accessory. Line chefs make good money, and they have a future, working their way up from shoving lasagna into the big ovens, picking up the secrets of the trade.

Danielle wasn't holding hands with him, but she was close to him, matching him stride for stride as they came through the swinging doors. Hugo sported a western-style belt and fake-pearl button shirts when he wasn't dressed in his chef whites. His cowboy boots made impressive clumping, scuffing sounds on the asphalt as he strode easily along, a little over six feet but only about 170, I guessed. A ballplayer build, tennis, soccer. We had always been friendly in a casual way.

"Hi, Steven," she said, hesitating politely in case I had anything I wanted to say. Giving me an open, serious expression, ready to talk, ready to listen. I had called her three times and didn't want to leave a message on the machine.

Hugo gave me a cool, easygoing, "Hey, Steven," and one of

those smiles you see in magazines, what fluoride can do for your teeth.

Danielle did give just a little bit of a glance back in my direction, a profile shot, disguising her curiosity by reaching up at the same time and fussing with her hair.

They left, walking along together, his arm touching hers, toward Hugo's metallic blue sport van. It was a new model, custom-detailed, with metal edge mudguards hanging behind the rear wheels, and sky blue curtains on the side windows, the kind that pull all the way shut.

CHAPTER FOURTEEN

I get nervous waiting.

So does my dad, but he covers it better, straightens pillows on the sofa, tells me what to wear.

"Liz says the elevator is working again," my dad said.

Dad had ordered my blue dress shirt washed with extra starch. It buttoned up stiff and unnatural, little creases starched into place releasing with soft sighs as I flexed my shoulders. The sleeves were too short for me, and I kept my elbows tucked in to disguise this. I put on pants I almost never wore, hairy wool, too tight around the middle.

Mom was late.

He had not told me, but I suspected that his plan had been for her to hear the piano as she approached our door. Maybe she would stand outside and listen to the music, rapt, thinking, Just like old times. Dad and I had not discussed it in every detail, but we both believed that Dad was going to win her back, get her to stay a few nights. Maybe she would develop the habit of staying around, finishing up her dissertation at home after she paid her parents her semiannual visit, down in the desert.

Henry the parakeet popped the mirror with his beak every

now and then, ringing the little bell attached to it. Every half minute or so the bird did it again, pecked his reflection. Every month or so he would decide to feed the mirror, smearing it with puked-up seeds. When I reached in to scratch his head, he closed his eyes in anticipation.

And then the yellow burst of energy was out of his cage, a flurry of wings, twice around the kitchen. He did a flying circus tour of the living room, as he did once or twice a month, when I changed his cuttlebone. With a whispered, miniature explosion of wings, he settled on top of my dad's head.

"How you doing, Henry?" said Dad, in a gentle, resigned tone. Dad had always lived with a pet of some kind, and after dinner in the right mood he'd unwind tales of cats rescued from avocado trees and stray dogs cured of mange.

He mouthed at me, as though he did not want to hurt the parakeet's feelings, "Put him back!"

Hard metallic raps, her key ring on the doorknob. I had expected her to have a key to the apartment.

I captured Henry just in time.

When you first see someone after a while they look different for a few heartbeats.

And then they look the same.

"The traffic was a disaster," Mom said, hugging Dad, hugging me, brisk, happy to be here, but nothing dramatic, like she had been gone for a weekend. She had left two years ago, living on the north coast. While she kept in touch through the fax machine and E-mail, she had not been in this apartment in months. "All the way through Pinole the freeway was packed like a junkyard."

Dad was explaining that he should call the restaurant, change our reservations, and Mom said she wasn't hungry.

You could see Dad's disappointment, so Mom corrected herself. "I can have a salad," she said.

"Are you okay?" she asked.

I said I was.

I could see her eyes searching my features for signs of boxing damage, puffiness, the kind of flattening and swelling that days will not erase. And if she had asked I would have told her this was part of the attraction—it was the kind of muscular competition her family loved, raised to a new order of danger.

"Steven's doing good," Dad said, a way of claiming responsibility for me that made it sound as though I was planning a career in sainthood, *doing good.*

"But Steven looks so—"

"He's growing up," said Dad, meaning: You should be around to see it.

Mom wears her hair tied up in a knot at the back of her head, and wears lace-up work boots, hiking boots, steel-toed, heavy-duty footwear. Her mother and father run a construction supply company near Barstow, selling tar paper and linoleum tile wholesale and retail, and Mom always dresses like someone prepared to hike into a quarry, her clothes well ironed and even attractive in a desert-warfare way.

"I guess that's it," she said. She touched her mouth, asking with her eyes what was wrong. "Why not football?" she had asked in an E-mail message months ago. "Why not basketball? Why boxing?"

"I did catch a punch on Monday. It healed up."

"Here, in the mouth," she said. "I can see it."

"It's okay."

"What's okay about getting slugged in the mouth?"

I gave a laugh, and said that the point is to avoid getting hit.

"You wish," she said, looking around at the furniture. My parents had agreed that I should live in East Bay with Dad because the schools were better than way out in the country, but I had begun to wonder if Mom might change her mind and invite me to move into an A-frame up north, somewhere close to a rural high school. I knew that if I waited long enough Mom would finish her dissertation and come home.

Dad had slipped into his well-worn Southwick tweed, and needed only a briar pipe to appear collegiate and gentlemanly, someone you'd pick out for an ad for single malt scotch. They both looked great. Dad didn't gaze off dreamily at his hands or at the view the way he often did. He concentrated on what Mom was saying, his head tilted forward, looking wide awake but at ease.

Mom rested her hand on the top of the piano, filling us in on what the tule elk were up to, overbreeding, filling up the acreage in Point Reyes National Seashore, needing birth control devices. If you put birth control chemicals in the water, other animals would drink it, with unpredictable consequences.

She tapped the piano's wooden surface, a string inside vibrating softly. Mom lived in a world of rock and talon. She liked to dance to music, and got vaguely restless sitting through all four movements of a symphony.

"The place looks good," she said.

I stooped and picked up a tiny yellow feather behind her back, over by the sofa.

Dad put his hands in his pockets, jingling coins, letting himself enjoy the compliment, maybe afraid to look at me or say anything abrupt, nervous that the rosy mood wouldn't last.

CHAPTER FIFTEEN

Dad had mentioned his choice of eating places the night before, wanting to know what I thought. Dad and I ate there once or twice a month—the choice was no surprise.

The veal was plastic, but no one in my family ate it anyway, since it comes from baby cattle kept in cages. I knew that the chicken was dry, but Mom likes that. She thinks if it's sinewy and hard to swallow it must be low-fat and practically health food.

If Mom enjoyed seeing the old sights along Solano Avenue she didn't say so. Dad had wiped out his passbook savings account to lease this sage gray Acura, sure that it would impress Mom. Our other car was parked on a side street near the apartment building, a Nissan sedan with foam rubber stuffing coming out of the dash.

Mom didn't complain, though, when Dad hunted for a place to park. He was not quite sure how to maneuver this car, bound to go back to the dealer in a few weeks. Mom could tell the car was a special effort to impress her, and she played along, getting the car stereo to play, adjusting the bass.

"Oh, this is nice," she said, in a friendly, Miss Manners voice, Dad holding open the door.

* * *

Dad cuts spaghetti with his knife and fork and doesn't roll it up on the tines, which I have always thought is one of the major joys of spaghetti eating. He's careful about little details, holding an extra napkin in one hand, dabbing at his lips after every other bite. He's even fussy about the bills he can't pay, keeping the credit card slips in tidy order in his wallet.

I couldn't come into a restaurant these days without realizing what it would be like to wash the dishes, and I eyed the orders of cannelloni being bused past, thinking—I bet that cheese sticks to the plate. The china was Homer Laughlin Seville, dishes that looked more expensive than they were.

"Daddy didn't come right out and say he needed me to help with the inventory," Mom was saying. "But I got the hint. Mom wants to help, but her cataracts are getting too bad. Years of desert UV radiation, I guess." The three of us used to go to Stinson Beach for picnics, and Mom would get excited if she saw a lesser scaup or a surf scoter or any other slightly uncommon bird. She was pleased once when I started keeping a life list of birds I had seen, trying to be just like her.

"What's there to inventory?" I asked. I had a dish of spaghetti and meatballs, Donofrio's a restaurant right out of a gangster movie. Coach Loquesto advised that pasta was an important food group, "a plate now and then," but that sugar was death. When I thought about my fight the next day my appetite withered.

"What's there to inventory," she echoed, a system she had patented, mocking you by repeating your words. "He sells blue-rock river gravel for forty years and you wonder what he has to count up before he can sell the business."

Dad took a long moment, tearing off a piece of the world's toughest garlic bread, but then he chimed in, "I thought your dad was organized."

My grandfather owns four skip loaders, a thirty-five-year old John Deere tractor, fire clay, Portland cement, gravel, river sand, bathroom grouting, forty pounds of wallpaper paste—which no one uses anymore—shelves of latex and high-gloss paint, and not only does it have to be counted up, you can't just throw stuff away and write it off as a loss on your taxes anymore.

At least, this is the story Mom told. "You have to have environmental protection experts," she concluded. "They come out all dressed up like astronauts and take away the gallons of paint thinner in a special truck."

"So he's retiring," said Dad, plunging ahead to the human element.

Her eyes were alight, and she leaned on her elbows, excited about counting ninepenny nails. Dad was already starting to look a little tired—she wears him out.

My grandfather was one more reason I felt compelled to learn how to throw a left hook. I had grown up hearing stories about how he played on the practice squad for the Chicago Bears: Tommy Carroway, wide receiver, too small to be able to take professional weight tackles, but a man who could chop wood twelve hours a day, swim the Russian River in full flood, and who had gone to Vero Beach to try out for the Dodgers four years in a row, as a third baseman, never quite making the team.

In recent years Grandpa had once surprised a burglar in the deluxe extra-wide trailer he and Grandma lived in at the edge of the desert. He hit the criminal with a straight right to the throat, and the man nearly died. Grandpa would tell the story when asked, whenever he visited, which wasn't that often—he was a busy man.

But you could see the tough-guy glint in his eye when he talked about landing the blow, and the glow of affectionate approval in Mom's, just as you could hear Dad's bland "Gosh what a story," and realize that this response did not measure up.

Dad had trouble with a renegade spaghetti noodle, and finally got it into his mouth. "Your Dad thinks every human being should wear a forty-five strapped to his hip."

My mother beamed at my father through her lashes, renewing a time-honored disagreement. "Daddy has liberal views on gun control," she said.

"Liberal, as in—the more firearms the merrier," said Dad.

"And what I was thinking, Steven," said Mom, giving me a sideways look. "Maybe you could come down and help out."

I took a sip of ice water.

My mother could see my surprise, and my reluctance, so she sidestepped. "Not tonight. Not tomorrow. But in the next few days. Fly down to Palm Springs—Daddy and I can pick you up, and you'll have a change of scenery."

I put down my fork. This was not the vision I had, Mom

staying in the desert day after day. I knew that if Dad could work the magic on Mom that he did on half the women in the East Bay, she would come back and live with us.

I said, "I'm busy with my boxing." I'm fighting a grown man named Stacy Martell tomorrow, I wanted to say.

You picture a man you are going to fight the next day very clearly, visualizing his nose and mouth and eyes.

Mom absorbed this, or made a show of it. Then she asked, "Are you and that new girl Danielle still . . ." She made a little loop-the-loop with her fork, signifying anything from friendship to a passionate love affair.

I had mentioned Danielle in my E-mail. "We're friendly," I said, matching Mom's ambiguity with some of my own.

"Ask about Raymond," said Dad, looking right at my mother, giving her a pointed instruction that won a level glance in return.

She took a few moments, touched a piece of bread into the olive oil on the plate before her, use-worn china, hard-to-break.

Then she asked, "How is Raymond?"

I explained that Raymond was still exercising out at the gym, pounding the speed bag, and maybe I was convincing, maybe I wasn't. My father had remarked to me that Raymond was developing a "furtive way" of looking around at things.

Dad smiled and put a hand out to touch hers. She took his hand, and there was something about the way she opened his palm and patted it, like someone about to tell a fortune, that gave me a little hope.

* * *

That night, alone in my room, I picked up my phone.

Danielle had a list of phone numbers, her pager, her computer line, her personal phone, her mom's. Danielle belonged to a golden retriever club, a swim club, a church group that sells chocolate, and a volunteer organization that visits people in the hospital. I called a couple of her numbers until I got her mom's voice on the answering machine again, telling me I had reached Binnie and Danielle.

I knew what must be happening, Danielle sitting there in the kitchen, screening calls, TV remote in her hand.

CHAPTER SIXTEEN

Did I hear a sharp burst of argument in the night? My father's snappy counterargument, pretending he didn't understand why she was mad at him? My mother restraining her shout with a whiplash whisper?

I made myself not hear my father explaining that he liked his friends—his women friends, especially—too much to let them go.

I tried to send them a thought, *calm down.*

The next morning I got up before dawn.

The kitchen was making little, meditative noises, the fridge humming, the electric clock on the wall counting down the seconds, a sound you would never notice in daylight. Henry was silent under his cover. My dad hated to throw anything away—the bird drowsed under an old pajama top.

It was a comfy lope to the crest of the hill, and then an easy pace back down again, four miles round-trip, saving plenty of stamina for today's three rounds.

I opened the front door quietly, not wanting to wake anybody.

I stumbled. My mom's duffel bag was there, right by the door, with a pair of hiking boots tied together, and a makeup kit, incongruously pink, with see-through stripes, lip gloss and eyeliner inside.

Dad was up, padding around in his sheik of Araby bathrobe, watching the coffeemaker dribble as though it absorbed all his attention.

"So," Mom said as I made my entrance. "The new Steven doesn't sleep until noon every day."

Much of the night I had watched videos with the sound turned to a murmur, respecting my parents' privacy. I have a small collection of championship bouts, mail-ordered from a catalog Loquesto loaned me, grainy black-and-white footage. The old-time boxers looked leaner and paler than modern men, their ears sticking out from their old-fashioned haircuts. In those days, when a boxer was hurt, his opponent hung on with one fist and pounded him with the other.

Mom briskly made small adjustments in her luggage, first aid kit, waterproof snack bag, the kind of travel equipment you could take into the Himalayas.

"You do this every morning?" Mom was asking.

I was busy using my mental antennas, sensing how things were between them. Surely she wasn't leaving right now.

Her question sounded simple, but I answered warily. "Run?"

"Run, that's what I'm asking."

"Just about."

"Maybe you're learning some discipline," she said.

Mom gives a compliment when she's about to slam-dunk

a criticism. Only a fool gets too pleased when she's being nice.

"It's good someone shows some maturity around here," she said.

Dad studied the coffee leaking into the pot.

"All you have to do is survive, Steven," she said. "Just another year and a few months and you'll be eighteen. You can come live with me then. We'll track black bears, do a coyote count, do some rock climbing. I look forward to it."

Her features softened. "I need it—I want to spend more time with you."

She was close to tears.

I stuffed her baggage into the cute little compact car, a Tercel, the lowest-mileage car she could find.

She took a deep breath and let it go, not a form of respiration with her, but a form of communication.

She said, "Think about coming down to see Gram and Daddy."

I told her I would think about it, finally giving her a little proto-smile, all I could manage.

I looked away for a moment, studying a long thin crack in the parking lot, subtle earth movement happening all the time, temblors we couldn't feel but only read about in the paper.

She flicked her gaze upward, toward the upper floors and our apartment.

"Some men never grow up," she said.

* * *

I watched her Tercel accelerate up the street, toward the overpass.

Mr. Torrance watched his dog force out a noodle of poop. I didn't want to go up to the apartment right then and listen to my father acting upbeat, reading lines from the *Chronicle* horoscope out loud, what kind of day we were going to have. Mrs. Torrance had waved her bejeweled pinkies at my mother—I don't know if Mom had waved back.

I didn't want to talk to anyone, but I didn't want to hurt their feelings.

Mr. and Mrs. Torrance must have had many questions about my mom and dad, whether my mother was going to move back here soon, where she was going right then. Mrs. Torrance had a sweet, courteous smile, and said that it was so nice to see my mother again.

"I bet your father is the happiest man in the world," said Mr. Torrance.

Mrs. Torrance knelt with a plastic bag, the task she was undertaking looking all wrong for her. She should have had a lady-in-waiting or a lab assistant to help her remove this dog stool from the pavement.

"With that new piano," Mr. Torrance was saying, making playing motions with one hand, the other gripping the leash, "I bet he has a ball."

This was the reaction my father always got—people who didn't know him very well caring about his state of mind. I could also see the unasked questions, the conversation this elderly couple was too polite to have right in front of me, why my parents couldn't get along.

"I used to play drums, myself," said Mr. Torrance, stepping hard on a half-smoked cigarette.

I tried to imagine this crisp, white-haired man hammering out a drum solo. I could very nearly envision him being in the army, in dress uniform, maybe playing drums for a color guard.

"I had a Ludwig drum kit, with a custom hi-hat a music shop over in Alameda ran up for me. Played jazz with a trio over in the city, in a little hole in the wall off Green Street. Never made much money at it, but we cooked."

I started to say that I thought he was an accountant.

"Harry was a very good drummer," said Mrs. Torrance with feeling.

"Tax preparation wasn't my whole life, Steven," he said, laughing that juicy, smoker's hack. But I wondered if maybe I'd hurt his feelings, acting surprised that he ever dreamed of anything but decimals and sacrifice bunts.

He said, "Everybody's got another side or two to their personality hidden away."

"It's a disappointment," was all Dad would say. Not *I'm disappointed* or *I bet you're disappointed, too.*

He was putting on a freshly laundered shirt and necktie, a dazzling blue silk, a new plan for the day already under way.

"She'll stop by on her way back," I said, half question, half statement.

He looked at himself in the mirror, his features oddly backward.

He said, "I don't know what's going to happen anymore."

I felt that I should say something to make him feel better.

But in the next breath he was asking me what I thought of his Robert Talbot tie, a present from a friend.

CHAPTER SEVENTEEN

Stacy Martell got out of his van in the gym parking lot. He didn't simply step down out of the vehicle—he swung himself out, one hand on the door frame, too muscular to move like a normal person.

He pulled out his gym bag, fussed with the van door, making sure it was locked. Raymond dug an elbow into my arm as we strolled across the parking lot, as though I would fail to see my opponent unzipping his bag, peeking inside, checking his pants pockets. Stacy was always a steady presence around the gym, signing up for cleanup duty, suggesting that we could bring our own towels to cut down on expenses.

"Lose something?" said Raymond, the sort of question timed to annoy rather than help, and hard to respond to—it sounds friendly, but it isn't.

Stacy's face folded into a smile. "Hi, you guys," he said softly.

Then Stacy took an extra moment and gave me a look side to side, up and down, almost the way a man will size up a woman. "I guess you're going to teach me some moves today."

"I'm here to learn from a master," I countered, just the right sauce on the words, *master* implying: veteran, old.

"Oh, you'll learn," he said.

I admired him, the way he respected and mocked me at the same time, guarding his composure. Even the way he betrayed his nerves, patting his pockets to make sure he had his car keys, was the right kind of double-checking. It's the one rule in boxing you never forget: protect yourself at all times.

He was square-headed, black-haired, sturdy, and fit. We strode along together, the three of us, and I couldn't help thinking that with his linebacker's neck and broad feet he would be hard to hurt. He had a six-year-old son going to Hawthorne Elementary School in Oakland, and a four-year-old girl he brought to the gym to jump rope in the shadows while he hammered the speed bag.

Raymond held the heavy steel door for us, making a little after-you gesture.

Stacy laughed, very quietly.

I wanted to delay the fight indefinitely.

The ceiling of the gym was darkness shot through with steel beams. Lamps hung straight down from the void, fluorescent racks too dazzling to look at.

Loquesto held the ropes wide so I could step through them. He huddled with Stacy, putting both hands on the man's shoulders, speaking directly into his face.

Then Loquesto sauntered over to me and gave me his full-face stare. "I'll tell you what I told him," he said. "Keep your punches up, and fight clean. Don't try to be a hero, if you get in trouble; we're not here to see you get hurt. You understand?"

He meant, Did I understand what he was saying and also

what he was not saying. He added something I suspected he had not told Stacy. "You're ready for this, Steven."

Del Toro was at ringside, in snakeskin cowboy boots and a western-style hat, chewing gum and giving me an upward nod as he caught my eye. He lifted his right hand and made a slow motion punch, as though to encourage me to calculate down to the millimeter where and how my own right hand would find its target.

Mr. Monday, the referee, clapped his hands together, getting Andy, the timekeeper's, attention, and an excited crowd gathered. No iron clanked in the weight room, and the machine-gun staccato of the speed bag was silent. Everyone was here, under the brightest lights, as close as they could get to the ring.

Raymond was attending my corner, and Mr. Monday said, "Hello, Raymond, how's your dad?"

Raymond had adopted an expression of artful weariness, as though nothing that happened here today would touch him. This was a lie, of course, but a boxer's seconds, his pals and cornermen, are supposed to look like that. Mr. Monday's pleasantry brought a different expression onto Raymond's face, a lively, sincere friendliness.

He said that his dad was doing great, still running goats.

Mr. Monday shook resin from a beanbag sack of the stuff, all over canvas near Stacy's corner, and he powder-puffed my corner, too. And then he looked around as though surprised to see everybody, and leaned against the ropes, letting his weight test the tension.

Mr. Monday and the timekeeper often talked about politics,

in a philosophical way. Andy was a senior at Hayward State University, a PE major, and brought *US News & World Report* along with his bag lunch. Mr. Monday's view was generally that life was complicated, while Andy felt that repealing income tax would solve every problem.

Now Andy was alert only to his boxing duties, testing the sports watch he wore around his neck.

At last I took a long look at my opponent, garbed now in a gray T-shirt and baggy sweatpants, jogging in place, his face compressed by the headgear and glistening from a coat of Vaseline.

"Go crazy," said Raymond, slipping through the ropes and down, out of the ring.

This was reasoned advice—Raymond had often discussed his theory that if an out-of-shape maniac fought a well-conditioned normal person, you had to give the odds to the insane combatant. The unpredictability and stamina of berserk behavior counted for a great deal, especially early in a fight, but I recognized that underneath Raymond's encouragement was another, worried message: Unless you fight like a madman, you don't have a chance.

Andy's wooden hammer sang off the bell.

Stacy, as though in an afterthought, slipped the mouthpiece between his lips. He made a chimpanzeelike grimace.

He waltzed across the ring, looking like someone who used to be able to ballroom dance and was testing out his footwork.

He hit me.

CHAPTER EIGHTEEN

I tried to hit him back, and I missed.

I had seen Stacy box often before, liking his peekaboo, step-by-step approach, the way he edged his opponent into a corner and then hurt him with left hands to the face.

It's even more disturbing when it's happening to you, his predictable left fist a jack-in-the-box that scored on my mouthpiece whenever he wanted it to.

The cartoon figures crowded around the ring howled, but I could not hear a sound. I had pictured this fight so vividly that I felt a confused boredom, the ropes whipsawing against my back as I ducked and yawed, my lower face going numb, my legs turning to water.

Raymond was shouting something, one hand crumpling his hair, one eye squinting, afraid to look.

It's always a jolt—how loud a punch is, and how much air it thuds out of the lungs.

I held on to Martell, a hand cupped around each of his shoulders, leaning into him, shoving him backward with all my weight. He took a half step back, and then shoved me all the way off, and snapped that jab after me.

I did it again—leaned into him, slipping jabs with my head, his leather glove making a squeak off my headpiece. I stayed on him, climbing to him, and he dug me in the ribs with both gloves, waiting for Mr. Monday to yell "Break!"

Mr. Monday barked, "Watch your heads," as our two cushioned skulls nearly collided.

Stacy swung at my sides, hooked into my belly, and I began retaliating, tight, self-protective little punches. A feeling of relief kept me where I was, letting Stacy punch me as hard as he could to the liver.

His punches were loud, with a little explosion of sound coming through his lips as he fought.

But he wasn't hurting me.

Not really.

I puzzled over this joyfully as I followed him, staying right in front of him as he backed up. He was treading steadily away from me. This quickened me, and I tackled him into the ropes.

"Get off him, Beech," said Mr. Monday, with the quietly irritated voice of a playground supervisor. "Box," he said. He meant: Don't wrestle.

But it's one thing to be cautioned or advised by the referee, and another to be warned. This was not a warning. Mr. Monday gave me a smile when I shot a peek at him. Mr. Monday bent forward like a baseball umpire who relished his work, and gave a back and forth movement of his head—keep fighting.

Martell adjusted his mouthpiece and stepped sideways, trying to matador me into the ropes as I charged into him. I swiveled on my toes and danced after him. He tried to keep me away with his left hand, and this was punishing for me, my jaw going numb again, my mouth filling with blood.

I landed a left hook to the face, and he dropped his hands for an instant, his legs locked at the knees. I couldn't believe my good luck—he was getting tired.

He jacked punches into me as hard as he could, but he was losing strength.

The bell clanked, Martell let his gloves drop again, and I gazed around like someone who had no idea what to do next, walk, sit, lie down. I knew what to do, where my corner was, but lack of oxygen made me feel stupid.

I forced a nonchalant look into my features and shrugged, a bit of theater. Raymond pried my mouthpiece from between my teeth and I said, "I'm all right."

"Spit in the bucket," said Raymond.

I was telling Raymond I felt great, and he was telling me not to swallow the blood, it would make me throw up.

"Spit!"

I spat into the blue plastic bucket, a tiny bit of red, and smiled, like I had done Raymond a big favor. Boxing does that, makes you glad for little things.

"You scared him," said Raymond.

I was about to tell Raymond that I thought I should throw more lefts, when the crowd changed, got a little quieter. The small audience parted, people with their hands in their pockets, talking over the first round, showing with little head movements how they would have slipped Martell's left.

A hush and a kind of social starchiness swept through the small knot of enthusiasts. Loquesto edged through the people, trying to intersect this stranger.

Chad was making his way to the ropes, gazing up at me, taller than I remembered, athletes and their girlfriends moving to get out of his way.

"It's okay," Raymond was saying to the coach, "he's with us."

Loquesto joined Chad beside the ring, leaned against it, ignoring Raymond, looking at Chad as though he had seen him before, probably asking if he had signed in at the front desk.

It was an unfriendly stare-off as Chad made a point of seeming to become aware of Loquesto, turned and looked right at him.

CHAPTER NINETEEN

The stare-off was brief, only a couple of seconds.

Then Loquesto climbed into the ring, and quickly went over to where Martell was leaning against the padded rung post, and gave a slow motion study of the left jab, how the fist rotates slightly as it extends outward, showing Martell he had to angle his feet to keep his body sideways, out of my reach.

I felt a little betrayed, Loquesto showing this experienced man how to neutralize me.

Loquesto came over to me. “Looking good, Steven,” he said.

“Chad’s a friend of mine,” I said.

Loquesto lifted one of his delicately scarred eyebrows. His expression said: No distractions.

He peeled down my lip, gave my cheek a pat.

“Score points,” the coach said. He meant: Throw more punches. You win a boxing match by being busy and active. Scorers pay attention to smart, telling blows; being tough doesn’t always win.

Sometimes you could catch Mr. Monday’s expression changing when he thought no one was looking. He would lean against the ropes, gazing outward, into the recesses of the gym, and he looked like someone enjoying a quiet day, waiting for promised tidings to arrive.

Then he would turn back, catch your eye, and hitch his features into an expression of avuncular no-nonsense, his inner joy a mystery.

The bell made its chime, and Martell did his tin-soldier waltz halfway across the canvas. I stayed on my toes, showing off, licking his headpiece with a couple of jabs, tempting him, and when Martell threw his right hand, his power punch, I was ready for it. I leaned to my left, like someone trying to see around a tall person, and rushed him, hanging on.

But this time I felt Chad's eyes on me.

And an inner voice nagged me, urged me forward. Have to win.

Have to.

But Martell had a new gambit, one that killed every attempt I made. When I hammered his ribs he grappled, smothering me, hugging me, pulling me nearly off my feet. Mr. Monday called for us to break, and finally had to reach in and pry us apart.

Several times we slow-danced like this, Martell's face an impassive, slightly smug mask, someone who knew the winning answer. Martell the boxer was nothing like Martell the helpful dad, willing to hold the stepladder while Mr. Monday screwed in a lightbulb.

Loquesto tells us to turn off the audience, like they aren't there. To Loquesto the gym is always empty, nobody home, just your opponent. He also cautions us never to have a casual conversation in the ring, never ask your opponent how he is, and definitely never ask anyone if they are hurt.

But all during the second round, and into the third, I was aware of Chad, even when I wasn't seeing him, the ringside faces a blur jerked this way and that by the body punches Martell threw, lefts and rights I tried to counter with uppercuts.

I felt the fight settle into a rhythm, Martell giving way, motoring backward, scoring with both hands, me bulldozing ahead, putting on a brave show, the sort of fight that could go ten rounds, no one getting hurt.

But I was a little tired, the long muscles of my arms and legs burning, the wind gasping in and out of me. Martell was trying to hang on. Midway into the third and last round, Martell shouldered into me. Standing sideways, he was able to flail at me with his left hand and circle.

Your arms get tired just holding the oversized gloves in front of your face, and my own arm bones were starting to ache. I was not surprised when Martell once again took a couple of long strides backward and let his gloves drop to his sides. He shook his arms, encouraging life back into them. I kept my chin down, feinted with a left, let him begin to raise his gloves.

I hit him with a right hand, a brilliant, picture-perfect blow. Right below the ribs, the punch you see in boxing highlights, an old-time champ stopping the action with one punch.

The people all around the ring seemed to catch this punch with him, a collective intake of breath.

Martell wore an anxious, tight expression.

He ducked toward me and I jacked a left uppercut into his chin, the point of his jaw digging all the way to my knuckles. I followed up with the same punch, but by then he had hit me once in the face, a pillow-soft punch. He was treading canvas far away from me, limping. He bent sideways, reaching down with his encumbered hand for his calf muscle.

I skewered a jab past the straight-arm left he was holding out in front of me. He was not boxing, now, grimacing, his leg buckling. Martell half-toppled, like someone doing a bad acting job, which is how people act when they are really hurt.

But he didn't go down. With Mr. Monday closing in, sure to end the fight because of Martell's leg cramp, Martell said he was all right.

It didn't sound like human speech, the words forced out around the mouthpiece, "I'm okay, I'm okay."

Mr. Monday motioned for us to continue.

Martell threw an illegal punch, a classic.

He hit me hard with an elbow, and did it perfectly, the point of his muscled arm right on my mouth.

I saw it coming, and so did everybody else but Mr. Monday.

I couldn't help it—my legs went out from under me. I sprawled. I couldn't get up, and Mr. Monday counted me out.

CHAPTER TWENTY

Smelling salts are worse than a slap.

One jolt and your eyes light up, your nervous system electrified by this chemical stun gun, your brain unable to believe any scent can be so sharp.

I was insulted, having Mr. Monday wave that stuff under my nose. I had not been knocked unconscious, not even for an instant.

Loquesto told me to sit on the stool in the middle of the ring and not get up for a while. I heard him tell Martell he was disqualified and that he ought to be ashamed of himself. "Really disgraceful," Loquesto said.

Martell's voice started in, an explanatory tone, and I heard Loquesto tell him to shut up.

Dr. Lu crouched down in front of me. He didn't bother asking me how I felt—boxers always lie. He beamed his tiny penlight into my pupils, looking around to see if my brain was hooked up. The illumination made me see a flash of blood vessels, the insides of my eyes. He held up his fingers. He asked me how many.

I spat blood into the plastic bucket. "Damn," said Mr. Monday, not swearing so much as commenting sympathetically. There was a lot of it.

Dr. Lu is a young doctor, with rimless glasses and a tendency to dress like an athlete, running shoes and polo shirts. He was a consulting physician for the Oakland Public Schools, and got free passes to games in exchange for being ready in case a basketball player fainted. Doctoring boxers was a hobby, or maybe an act of goodwill.

He said I needed a stitch or two in my lip. "It will take a matter of seconds," he said. He told me to drop by his office, a block or two away, next to the tuxedo rental shop on Broadway.

"Good fight, Steven," said Del Toro as I passed him on my way toward the locker room. "Next time he's a dead man."

I couldn't look in Chad's direction.

Raymond didn't talk until after I had showered and had my street clothes on. I dabbed on some of the stolen aftershave, examining my face in the mirror. The bridge of my nose had been barked, not bloody so much as angry, a red place where there used to be normal flesh.

The inside of my lip didn't have a cut, just a little rent, as though my mouth was growing a new duct.

"You did really well," Raymond said at last, sounding quiet and tired. "You had power in both hands. Martell cheated and he got caught."

I was in no mood for conversation.

Loquesto entered the locker room, letting his arms dangle the way even ex-boxers do, staying loose.

He said, "You're going to San Diego."

The news dazzled me, but it confused me, too. I knew I hadn't done that well today.

Loquesto sat down beside me, Raymond looking on, his eyes tense, hopeful.

Loquesto said, "You'll have to come up with the registration fee, the airfare, the hotel. I'll write you in as our number one middleweight novice."

I could not speak until I cleared my throat. "I should have finished him when I had the chance."

"If your opponent fights dirty, what can you do?" Loquesto rubbed the back of his head. "I got a rabbit punch in Cannes one night—I can still feel it. It was the only time I ever fought in Europe, one sneak punch in the fifth round and I was looking at the ceiling. I had a great left hook that night. *Crochet de gauche,* they call it."

"But you lost the fight," I said.

"I won. My opponent was disqualified."

I thought about this, and considered Loquesto in a new light, someone who had gone further as a pro than I had guessed.

"San Diego trip comes to six hundred dollars," he said. "With insurance. If you can't afford it—"

"My dad can write a check."

Loquesto didn't speak for a moment. Then he added, "There are church groups and YMCA donations that'll cover the costs. Most boxers can't cough up the money."

I told him I didn't need any help.

* * *

Stacy was lingering in the hall, and saying he was sorry, that it was one of those things.

Raymond walked stiffly and wouldn't even look at him.

Stacy looked like a security guard with two kids again, solid, pink-cheeked, as though he had been jogging around Lake Merritt, not trading punches.

I gave him a nod, staying silent, and patted his arm, because I understood.

I knew how to cheat, too.

CHAPTER TWENTY-ONE

"I am not going to park this car right in front of the restaurant," said Chad.

Raymond was driving, switching on the turn signal to make a left turn, Oakland serene in afternoon sunlight, brick buildings and Victorian gables. Some of the old buildings had been repainted and outfitted with flower boxes, pink geraniums. Nobody looked in a hurry, all the pedestrians in a good mood.

I had dropped by the doctor's office. The doctor was there ahead of me, opening his mail. He had used a cotton-tipped wooden swab to paint my inner lip with painkiller, a flavor like spearmint mouthwash. I closed my eyes and felt the needle, the duct getting sewed up tight. I had asked Dr. Lu if the cut would hurt my career, and he replied, "Not a cut like this."

"They have parking in the back," said Raymond, easing the car along at a leisurely pace.

"The first thing a cop does when he goes on duty is check out the cars parked behind Camino Real," said Chad.

"This is a shiny white Pontiac," Raymond said. "It's going to be visible, no matter where we park."

Chad leaned forward. "Park along in here."

I had assumed we were seeking a shadowy alleyway. This was a highly visible street with gleaming parking meters, the three of us searching our pockets to come up with enough coins.

Camino Real is a restaurant right across the street from the Oakland Police Department. My father and I used to eat there after hearing the Oakland Symphony. Once we had seen a man get arrested there, spread out on the floor, cuffed, propped upright, and marched out the door, no fuss, no complaint. Dad had shaken his head, taken a forkful of *refritos*, and said, "How about that?"

Turning back to survey the street, the last thing you see is the tall tower of detention cells for arrested suspects. People in Camino Real have the street-scruffy look of plainclothes detectives, or guys who have just dropped by after seeing their brothers and sisters in jail.

Chad gave the place a good look, eyeing the booths under the far wall painted with pictures of Mayans working on their cities, and he picked out a place in the corner, a view of who came and went.

"Steven coldcocked that security guard," Chad said, picking out the largest tortilla chip and popping it into his mouth. He had laughed when Raymond told him that Stacy was a guard for American Security. "One punch, and that night watchman was a cripple."

"The man got a leg cramp," said Raymond. "Steven fought well, but what happened was his opponent got a muscle spasm and had to throw a dirty punch to survive."

"I was there," said Chad.

"You were there, but maybe you don't have that much—" Raymond stopped himself before he said *knowledge about boxing.*

Chad let Raymond know he could hear the words that were said, and the ones Raymond kept to himself. "I don't think I have a high opinion of the sport," said Chad. "But I understand someone who can knock out a rent-a-cop."

Chad offered me a sly look of sympathy—almost pity—and Raymond held a tortilla chip in his fingers, not eating. The painkiller was wearing off and I could move my mouth. It hurt, but not very much.

"Loquesto maybe did one thing right in his life," Chad continued, "teaching Steven how to box. It's a shame about Loquesto, maybe the man had some ability. He turned out to be one of these guys running away from his past."

There was, in fact, a touch of the fugitive in the way Loquesto kept stacks of fresh dress shirts, starched and waiting, next to his collection of sports magazines in the office, as though he might have to don a new disguise any minute. Maybe feinting and dodging in the ring makes you believe in a fluid sneakiness you can't shake off when you retire. But I didn't want to hear any criticism of the coach, and maybe Raymond didn't either.

Raymond said, "Loquesto's not such a jerk."

Chad let this affront pass like it hadn't been uttered. "I used to shoot baskets, play one-on-one with my brother until it was too dark to see."

For a moment I could see the boy Chad sitting there, although I wondered if he might suggest a game between the three of us, a chance to use his height and experience.

"Did you play basketball in school?" I asked, expecting him to make some dismissive remark about education.

"I wasn't good enough at the game," he said.

"It takes practice," I said, a little surprised.

He happily admitted that this was so. "But even with practice I was only going to be pretty good, not serious-good."

Chad talked about how he had gone fishing with his brother once, and how his brother caught a perch right out of the bay. I was very hungry, eagerly awaiting the arrival of my *flautas con guacamole.* When an unshaven, convict-type customer looked my way, I gave him a stare until he found something else to do with his eyes.

I felt the stitches with the tip of my tongue, like a huge sailor's knot. Our food arrived, gigantic Syracuse china platters, with food baked onto the surface so thoroughly I had to imagine the hydraulic power in the dishwashing arena, real pros gunning frijoles off the dishware.

"This is a wonderful sight," said Chad, and he delivered up a smile aimed right at the waitress, beaming up at her like a man who had never seen such a beauty in his life. She was good-looking, pretty eyes and plenty of chest. Her arrival broke Chad's mood.

"Hot plates," said the waitress. "Don't burn your fingers."

Chad waited for her to leave, and rolled his eyes at us, letting us imagine what slurs he was silently casting in the waitress's direction, *pussy, slut.*

There was no way I could borrow money from Chad.

I tested my mouth with a tortilla chip. The salt scalded my cut lip, but I maneuvered the food around so it didn't sting much.

Raymond stirred his chili sauce with his fork, not eating.

I listened, and as I did I thought: If I don't go along with these two, they will get themselves shot. Or worse yet, maybe they wouldn't do anything at all, maybe just talk about it.

There was no way I could ask my cash-strapped dad for the money, and I wasn't about to call my mom that night and steer the conversation around to how much it costs to make it in amateur sports.

I was going to have to take a risk.

CHAPTER TWENTY-TWO

Outside our apartment you can sometimes hear conversation, even when you can't make out the words, a rise and fall of sounds, unmistakably human, but obscure.

I thought my mother had come back.

I took a moment before I opened the door, listening to my father's voice and a woman's. The key slipped almost soundlessly into the slot.

A woman who looked nothing like my mother, a petite, well-coiffed woman, was perched on the sofa. She looked at me with wide eyes, like someone startled. Dad often invited his women friends here, but I had expected him to take a vacation from this habit for a few days, out of respect for Mom's visit.

This woman certainly didn't dress like my mother, wearing a puffy-sleeved concoction, dark, creased pants, and the kind of shoes that look dressy, except they have Vibram soles with serrated treads—you can walk nine miles to the office.

Dad was sitting beside her, a folder open on his lap, receipts and business forms all over the coffee table. He glanced up and smiled, a brighter, happier man than the shell I had left this morning.

The woman ran her hands up her arms to keep the overlarge

sleeves from slipping down, younger than Mom, and someone who paid more attention to her looks.

Dad stirred himself out of whatever airy mood he was in and said, "Steven, this is Emily Shore."

She was a voice I recognized from the phone, the husky, slow-speaking financial advisor. She had quite a grip, and plainly put some effort into it, letting me know she was used to shaking hands with big bucks.

"I'm so glad we could meet at last," she said, low and careful, someone who had trained herself out of a hometown accent. She had more of a figure than my mom, and maybe the stylish parachute-blouse was a way of disguising this, keeping the male mind on the bottom line.

"I'm going to give piano lessons," said Dad.

I said I was glad to hear it. Actually, Emily Shore seemed nice enough, but I knew it was pointless to get friendly with the women Dad brought home. A few turns of the calendar and Dad would have a replacement.

"Emily says we can write off the rent we pay on fifty percent of the unit," Dad was saying. You could see what women saw in him, his enthusiasm for the subject at hand, whatever it was.

A single plate with crumbs gleamed in the breakfast nook. Two cups of chamomile tea, three-quarters gone, the tea bags sitting soggy in the sink. The tea was cold. The carpet is so new you can see the footprints, ghosting here and there down the hall, toward the bedroom.

"We can write off cookies and coffee for the piano students, and a percentage of the rent on the furniture," Dad was saying, picking up sheet music company invoices like they were long-lost family letters. "We're taking a proactive tax strategy."

"A tax strategy," I said, trying out one of Mom's dry echoes.

Couldn't you work things out better with Mom? I wanted to say. You had to call up this living ad for eye shadow and ask her to drop by to discuss how to avoid paying taxes on a gaunt income?

The way I stood there got Dad's attention—he isn't stupid—and when he swings into full focus you know it.

He said, "Where have you been?"

"Stacy Martell," I said, being truthful but not elaborating. I gave a hint, making a fist.

Emily made a self-conscious stretching movement, maybe embarrassed and letting off a little tension, Dad and son about to have a set-to right in front of her.

Dad's features softened. "Steven boxes."

A very un-Momlike dimple appeared in Emily's cheek. "You told me," she said.

"But I mean he *boxes*. You ought to see him move the big bag around."

Dad had never come to see me in one of my bouts, explaining that he was 100 percent behind me but couldn't bear to look.

"Really?" said Ms. Shore, one of those exclamations that mean either *how fascinating,* or *I have no idea what you mean.*

"The 'big bag' is that huge leather sausage you see boxers pounding in movies," Dad explained. "Boxing is full of droll terminology. A guy who gets cut a lot is called a tomato can. When you hear that a fighter has fought a string of easy opponents you say he's been fed a diet of dead bodies."

"Good heavens," said Emily, sounding sultry and polite in a way that made it easy to see why Dad might want to tell her all kinds of things.

"Dad has read a couple of books about it," I said.

"How'd the match go?" Dad asked, not getting it quite right. Soccer teams and chess players have matches.

"He extended me," I said. I was being deliberately technical, using a boxing term for "he gave me a challenging workout."

I really wanted to ask my father what had gone wrong. He spent the night with my mother and got up the next day with nothing to say for himself. I wondered if maybe all women were the same for Dad, no matter the differences in their faces or their views on life.

"I'm designing a poster," said Dad, proud, like this was a rare talent for an intelligent adult.

Ms. Shore handed me a blue sheet of paper. My dad looks good in all his photos, carefree, lively. *Beginners welcome. Piano study with a master. Hourly rates.*

I said, "Maybe it should go 'Study piano,' instead of the other way."

"That's what I thought," said Ms. Shore, giving me a ninety-dollar smile.

My bedroom is not a place to spend a long evening alone.

I have a TV and a video player, and some paperbacks I keep

around, but it's been years since that morning I saw an African lion sitting in the sun. I kept my ancient comic book collection in a Ballantine scotch box, and I had shelves of rocks and curiosities I had once found interesting, a penny that had been run over by a switch engine in the Oakland rail yard, a .45 shell I had found in a creek bed, a rattlesnake rattle my mother's father had sent me in a Jiffy bag.

I called up Danielle and got her mother, the mega-nurse. Binnie is very cheerful on the phone, the way people are when they talk to five hundred voices a day. She said could she take a message, and, no, Danielle hadn't mentioned me. Binnie wished me a good day even though it was night.

Raymond had told Chad, point-blank, that nobody would get hurt, and Chad had put his hands up in easy surrender.

He said it was the last thing he wanted.

CHAPTER TWENTY-THREE

I still had a couple of hours before I was supposed to meet Chad and Raymond, and I looked out at the hills going Easter pink with sunset, the sun out of sight on the other side of the building.

I wondered what I was supposed to wear on a night like this. Chad had said "something dark," but I wondered: Sweatpants? Jeans? I had trouble picking out a shirt, too, every color too bright.

I could hear my father out in the living room, demonstrating to Ms. Shore how even a tax strategist can learn the triplets in "Moonlight Sonata."

The clock was not moving.

I called my grandparents and the phone rang and rang. My grandparents were the first people in North America, probably, to have an answering machine, decades ago, so I wondered what the problem was. Or maybe they were out under the desert twilight, drinking iced tea and letting the barbecue coals get that nice, even char.

A male voice answered on about the eleventh ring, my grandfather.

"Girlie and Gram are off looking at the yucca trees," he said.

That's what he calls my mom, *Girlie*. There had been a son, my uncle, who died of meningitis before his first birthday. My grandfather likes to sneak up and grab you from behind and then laugh. He really used to scare me when I was little.

I wanted to ask if the yucca trees had been doing something unusual, vanishing only to reappear in strange places. I offered some general remark, about how stunning the landscape was. "But hot," I added, feeling ridiculous, making the most vapid small talk in history.

"She's doing just great," said my grandfather, meaning: Mom looks fine without your dad in her life. "But we're all set to see you," he added.

Maybe I had hidden a hope from myself—that I might blurt out that I needed money, that I would love to come down and drive a rusted-out pickup truck up and down the desert acres.

A part of me would have loved double-pumping the clutch on an old Dodge four-wheel drive, but at the same time I heard the challenge in my grandfather's voice, the macho drill bit as he went on to say he'd let off both barrels of his twelve gauge right at a coyote the week before, and blew a hole this big.

"How big?" I asked, playing along the way my dad does, sounding boyishly amazed but actually waiting for the conversation to be over.

"About as big as a grapefruit," he said. And then I sensed the age in him, the uncertainty, questioning himself. "Or maybe a little smaller, about like an orange. I don't know. I missed with the other barrel," he said, his voice trailing off.

I said that I didn't realize you could hunt coyotes, chiding myself silently for challenging him even in this oblique way.

"Oh, hell, Steve," he chuckled. "The fence was what I blew out. I missed the coyote by about a half a mile."

He laughed and laughed, enjoying my confusion, or maybe amused at his own failed bravado, blasting a gap in some old redwood planks.

My mom sounded years younger. "Oh, it's so wonderful to drink water right out of a well," she said.

Then, "When are you coming down?"

In old-time boxing matches, if you got cut or woozy the referee didn't stop the fight like they do now. The boxers fought on, ribbons of black streaming down their faces in the old silver-and-gray films, the fighters not seeming to mind, like they were already legends, or ghosts.

I stalled as long as I could with my videos.

At last it was time.

CHAPTER TWENTY-FOUR

The Blockbuster Video parking lot was cold.

Chad was walking in a loop, like a pitcher circling the mound. Raymond stayed within himself, hands in the pockets of his dark pants, his long shirtsleeves fluttering in the wind. I was wearing forest green pants, with a loose-fitting, long-sleeved sweatshirt against the chill.

Dad had finally finished showing off his piano fingers, giving the Bechstein a workout. He had knocked on the bedroom door, his signature tip-tap, to announce that he and Ms. Shore were heading over to the city to hear an old mentor of Dad's, a jazz pianist. "I'll be back by midnight," he said. I told him I had a late shift at the cafeteria, and would be back by two.

"You hungry?" I asked Raymond.

I was stalling, not wanting to begin just yet.

"Not really," Raymond responded, keeping his body at an angle to the wind. Then he added, "Chad heard from his sister-in-law today."

I began to ask right away—what happened? But then I sensed bad news and I didn't want to hear another word.

Raymond rubbed his hands together, keeping them warm, and popped them back into his pockets. "She filed her divorce papers this week," he said.

I was almost relieved that the news wasn't something worse.

Chad opened the front passenger door and got in, one hand slapping the dash, looking back at us, a show of impatience.

"Plus, his brother got hurt today," said Raymond in a low voice.

Chad put a head out of the car, gesturing, *Do I have to wait all night?*

"In the prison yard," Raymond continued softly. "A shiv in the back. He'll be okay, but Chad's—" I could sense Raymond trying to select the right words. "He's not in a very good mood."

We got into the car. Raymond started the engine, and glanced back at me.

I offered a reassuring smile. Maybe he could see it.

"I might be able to eat a pizza slice," Raymond offered.

"We'll eat after," said Chad, his voice hard and quiet. He reached under the seat and brought out a bottle of Bacardi rum, three-quarters full. He screwed off the top and drank. The liquor sloshed in the bottle and gave off a sweet-sick smell.

Raymond drove carefully. I sat in the back, watching the slow lights and traffic, all of it too quiet, car doors slamming, people talking, without a sound.

The liquor store on the corner of Washington and San Pablo sells lottery tickets and sparkling water, canned veggies and fingernail clippers. Bottled liquor gleams on the shelves behind the cash register. The place was a box of white light, fluorescent glow in every corner, SHOPLIFTERS WILL BE PROSECUTED in red letters.

The sign in the front window said MONEY ORDERS, which Chad said meant they have bundles of twenties and fifties sitting in a box somewhere. I had borrowed a little cash from Raymond, so I could make a purchase like a customer.

The white Firebird was across the street, lights off, although you could see vague shapes in the darkened interior. My own reflection stared back at me from the glass.

Magazines showed off female body parts over on one corner, by a stack of horse-racing tabloids. You could buy Pres-To-Logs, cat food, marmalade. A woman paying for a pack of Marlboro Lights spoke with the man behind the counter, laughing.

Raymond had flashed me a don't-leave-me glance as I left the car. A fish-eye mirror high up in one corner showed a weird, wide-angled view of shelves of jug wine and California champagne. A video camera with a tiny red eye peered down from above a display of lemon-flavor Calistoga water.

The proprietor was starting to watch me, smiling with his customer, but craning his neck as I searched up one aisle of bottled wine and down another. If he had a weapon it was behind the counter, not up on the wall like a trophy shotgun or a hunting rifle, deterrence for all to see.

The owner was watching me now with his full attention.

What struck me just then was that it could be done. Not now, not this way, but if all you wanted was to knock out one cash-fat till, grab the currency, and run, it wouldn't be that difficult.

This insight made me feel all the more innocent. I could do harm, and yet I wouldn't. I was like a boxer in a position to hit a defenseless opponent, holding back.

It would work, if you did it right.

It would be easy.

CHAPTER TWENTY-FIVE

I put on an act, relieved to find what I was looking for, digging my hand into my front pocket.

I paid for a can of salted peanuts, counting out my change, really more than I wanted to spend, and dodged traffic across the street.

"Only if we wore masks," I said, slamming the car door.

"Masks," said Chad. He screwed the cap back onto the liquor bottle.

"We could put them over our heads," I said.

If robbery was going to work you'd need two men, I reasoned, not three, or best of all, just one man with a weapon that he could brandish. Freeze the counterman, paralyze the customers with shock, crack the till, grab the money, and show what weeks of running every morning can do for the legs.

It was almost a good plan. I had that feeling you get when you let your fists drop and dare an opponent to hit you. You feel untouchable, and there is nothing he can do.

Chad put a forefinger to one eyebrow, scratching his face, his posture communicating disapproval. "You saw the video camera?" I could smell the booze on his breath, and I wondered how stupid rum makes people.

"One. But the guy behind the counter could see you sitting out here."

"So we'll go get us some bags," said Chad. "Brown paper ones, not plastic, three nice bags."

Chad turned his head to see in my direction in the backseat, but looking beyond me, too, at the street. Raymond was too preoccupied with inner thoughts to do more than key the ignition, start the engine, the Firebird idling a little rough.

"We can each buy something," Chad was saying, "at Safeway up the street, ask for paper not plastic, and poke eyeholes out with our fingers."

"This liquor store owner," I said, "is going to let three guys walk in off the street with brown paper bags over their heads?"

I let the question hang there, no further comment necessary.

"What's he going to do, Steven?" Chad said. *Stee-ven* like he was mocking it in some way.

He'll call 911, I was about to respond, but then I figured I had made my point. "The plan is okay," I said, careful not to offend, "but we can tweak it a little. We need a better store. And leave Raymond in the car."

Chad examined my purchase, shaking the can of salted nuts, prying off the lids, one plastic, one metal with a pull ring, and the car filled with the fragrance of roasted nuts.

We ate mixed nuts for a while, the three of us chewing. Then Chad put the blue plastic lid over the can, carefully, and placed the can beneath his seat. He wiped his hands on his shirt front, then leaned over and hit the glove box.

He rustled among papers in the dark interior. He pulled out a handgun.

He examined the automatic, holding it in the flat of one hand, continuing to wipe his other hand on his pant leg.

Raymond shrank over against the driver-side door, putting his hand on the parking brake, releasing it very slowly. I didn't move, sitting there without making a sound. In the store across the street the owner was a silhouette, torso and head.

Raymond looked back, the way the drivers do in the training videos, making sure there was no oncoming traffic.

We drifted out onto San Pablo Avenue, passed an auto body shop, a Beverages and More outlet, and then Chad said, "Make a left at the light, go around the block. Sit up behind the wheel, Raymond, or I'll have Steven drive."

At the red light Raymond looked back at me, a nice tight little smile, both wondering and a little scared. Because with Raymond you always sensed an undercurrent. He didn't care, and he cared a lot. I tried to send him a mental message, that it would be all right.

He made just the tiniest little shake of his head, his eyes on mine.

I cleared my throat. I didn't want to say the wrong thing, not sure how strongly the liquor was working on Chad. I was also not used to being in a car with a handgun.

"What kind of gun is that?" I asked, like it was easy, controlling the unsteadiness in my voice.

CHAPTER TWENTY-SIX

"This is a Browning Hi-Power nine millimeter," Chad said, matter-of-fact. He put it up over his headrest, like I might not believe him, holding it where any passing car could see.

The gun had a very subtle odor, all the way in the backseat. Oil and metal, mixing with the smell of the rum.

I had to keep myself from shivering.

"It's been chopped down," he continued, studying the weapon, "the rear sight taken off and the grip shortened. I keep a round chambered."

His description of the Browning was delivered in a tone new to me. Chad was either quoting his older brother, someone with full command of language and mechanics, or else the act of holding a gun gave him new authority.

The street was under repair, Solano Avenue a battlefield of piled-up dirt, the pavement uneven. Raymond made a turn, and we drove by sleepy houses.

"So we're going to walk into this liquor store with this big greasy pistol and our heads in bags." I couldn't keep my voice from trembling, trying to be sarcastic, but surprised at how I really felt.

The gun made it even easier, if I was crazy enough to go ahead with this.

Chad cocked his head. "It's not greasy," he said quietly, no-nonsense, the way Coach Loquesto could sound when he felt like it.

I was about to say that this kind of store owner always has a shotgun under the counter. At the same time I realized that we were very close.

We were very close to doing it.

"What's that funny noise?" demanded Raymond.

"Steven clearing his throat," said Chad.

Raymond said, "No, there's a rattling under the hood."

We all made a show of listening, eyes gazing at some point in the distance, the way people do when a sound steals their attention.

"The engine's acting up," Raymond said. He pulled over to the curb.

An ATM across the street was bright in the streetlight, a metal front with a black computer screen and a metal slot for twenty-dollar bills.

Chad had one hand out to the dash, looking back to me for an explanation.

"Fuel pump," I suggested.

Raymond shook his head, then lifted a hand off the wheel: Maybe.

Chad put his hand on the steering wheel, sensing the car's vibration.

A man with a small, square dog shuffled from a car with its

headlights on, a woman at the steering wheel. He had trouble walking, each step hesitant, reaching for the wallet at his hip. As he glanced across the street in our direction, he took a long moment, memorizing the make and license number of the Pontiac.

"Cautious man," said Chad. "Wrapping his leash up tight, protecting his dog from getting stolen."

The man drew his dark, jumpy little dog in close, hunching protectively before the ATM machine, and Chad chewed a fingernail, laughing without sound. "Look, the dog is cold," he said as the mutt nosed the air in our direction.

"Those small dogs are always like that," said Raymond, as though relieved to find a neutral subject for conversation.

"Always afraid of being killed," said Chad.

"We can't go back to the liquor store," I said. "That owner could paint our portraits. What we need to do is find another store that sells money orders, a new place, wear bags, and make sure the guy behind the counter sees the gun."

The car was idling fast.

"He has to see the gun," I said. "Just set eyes on it. That's all." Meaning: No harm to anyone.

Chad licked his upper lip slowly, someone doing calculations in his head.

Right then I realized what Raymond was doing, subtly stepping on the clutch, tickling the accelerator, giving it too much gas, trying to make the car sound bad.

Chad put his hand on Raymond's shoulder with artful gentleness.

"Drive right," Chad said.

* * *

In daylight, going into Safeway for groceries is a routine but pleasant experience, selecting a cart, pushing it along through the aisles. You can start with fruits and veggies, sniffing the cantaloupes, or you can head right over to the other end of the market, to the red meat.

At night it doesn't feel right, all those shiny labels. The three of us looked shadowy and sleepless, although Chad held up best under the bluish glare of the lights, sauntering along like a man with a memorized grocery list, picking out a box of raisins.

"We'll all go shopping together," Chad had said, sticking the automatic under his shirt, and now I had the feeling he was going to do it right here.

Here at the express checkout.

I tried to flash him a mental message: *No.*

I caught Chad's eyes and he gave me a reassuring uplift of one corner of his mouth. He shook his head, filled with a secret amusement, as though picturing cash all over this tiled floor, security guards running from all directions. He let his gaze wander absentmindedly over the display of Snickers and Mars bars near the checkout, looking like a man just off work starving for raisins and peanut butter, the purchase he was about to make.

Raymond stood like a person demonstrating bad posture, hunched over in another line, holding a box of powdered milk and a jar of French's mustard. Raymond counted money out of his wallet. I was the only one who had chosen a living object, a very large Crenshaw melon.

CHAPTER TWENTY-SEVEN

Raymond drove along San Pablo Avenue, past the Albany Police Department and Church's Fried Chicken, proceeding with exacting care.

"Right there," said Chad, a liquor store passing by on the opposite side of the street.

"There's a cop," said Raymond.

"I don't see anyone," said Chad.

"I saw a policeman in the store as we went by," said Raymond.

"There's no cop unit parked outside, Raymond," said Chad.

Raymond set his jaw.

Chad let his silence fill the car, staring at the side of Raymond's face, the muted hues of turn signals and businesses flowing over us.

"Was this an Albany cop?" Chad asked after a moment. "Or was it a Berkeley cop? Or was it a security guard?"

Raymond made an impatient hiss through his lips. "I saw him with his gun and his badge, and where you see one—"

"'Where you see one,'" Chad echoed.

Raymond lifted himself up and resettled himself in the front seat, shaking his shoulders.

"Maybe Raymond's right," I said, "and maybe he isn't. It doesn't matter."

Chad gave me an incredulous look, shadows shifting across his features.

"We don't want to take unnecessary risks," I said.

Chad waited, letting me talk.

I said, "Let's take the freeway up to Richmond."

Every traffic light was green, for blocks. The storefronts were all dark and empty. We took a right on University Avenue, and headed toward the interstate.

As we passed the hulks of parked cars Chad put a hand out to Raymond's sleeve, and Raymond slowed down. Chad rolled down the side window, studying a Toyota pickup parked under a streetlight.

"The owner's asking to have his little truck stolen," said Chad. "Leaving it out here in this empty place."

But that tightness in me was gone. I could feel it now—nothing was going to happen. We had come close to walking into a wine and beer shop with a gun, and we didn't do it.

"Drive up the on ramp," said Chad.

We were out of danger.

I felt like laughing, amazed at how close we had all come.

I offered a prayer of thanks.

"Go up on the freeway," said Chad.

The Firebird spat gravel from the rear wheels, good traction, as Raymond aimed the car up the on ramp, onto Interstate 80.

The acceleration was pulling us back into our seats when we saw the stalled car beside the freeway.

It was perched on the side of the road, a subcompact with its hazard lights pulsing. The outline of the small car was obscured by vapor or smoke. A figure stood well away from the vehicle.

A woman waited, arms wrapped around herself in the dark, the flashing hazard lights illuminating her rhythmically as we passed her, her coat fluttering in the breeze from the bay and the swirling air in the wakes of the big trucks.

Chad put the back of his hand on Raymond's sleeve, just his knuckles, almost an affectionate gesture. The Firebird swung over onto the shoulder of the freeway. We braked hard, the three of us straining against the forward momentum, trucks rumbling past, their tires banging over a seam in the highway.

Chad said something to Raymond, and Raymond reversed the Firebird, all the way back to the silver-gray Sentra. Raymond avoided meeting my eyes, frowning with concentration, having trouble keeping the Firebird on an even course, driving backward with weeds and litter popping and thrashing under our wheels.

Chad was out of the car without a word.

I jerked the door handle, and spilled out into the night air, the wafts of diesel dust and bay wind fluttering my clothes.

Gouts of coolant-flavored steam swept over me, and the vapor parted as two people, Chad and the woman in a fluttering raincoat, came toward me, their steps crunching the gravel and glittering glass.

Chad was hanging on to her, one fist around her arm, her hand flailing with each step, flopping, her face bent back to protest, or to record Chad's features. Her purse slapped the side of her raincoat as he dragged her the remaining steps, and then she lurched and tried to run.

She went nowhere.

She kicked Chad, her dark slip-on shoe catching sand and trash that muffled her attack, and so it was only the second kick that really found meat and bone. He made a quiet sound. He stuffed her into the backseat beside me as I scooted over.

She clawed him, caught his face with her fingernails, her mouth twisted, making noise.

But not nearly enough, her scream raspy, and then when she found her voice, it was captured by the interior of the car. Chad jabbed at her with the muzzle of the handgun, methodically, like someone breaking the glass out of a window frame, hitting her in the face.

CHAPTER TWENTY-EIGHT

There was not enough air in the car.

Raymond held on to the steering wheel with both hands. The car squealed and made a shrugging, sideways sweep into the flow of traffic. The match-head whiff of burned rubber filled the car for a few seconds.

Chad had gotten back in the front seat, and I was sitting right next to the woman.

Chad rasped directions into Raymond's ear.

We left the freeway, approaching a traffic light.

Too fast, I thought.

We're going too fast.

The woman's raincoat spread all over the backseat, half falling off her. I was sitting on a sleeve and a long, loose cloth belt. She had her hand over her mouth, like someone appalled at what she had just said, embarrassed.

I wanted to say something reassuring.

She had blond hair, pulled back in a loose ponytail, strands slipping out, straying over her face. She wore a white or cream-colored blouse under her coat, starred with blood. Her purse, a well-worn eel-skin bag on a stout strap, was gaping.

The Firebird careened through a yellow traffic light, Raymond struggling to pull the car to the left. Chad and Raymond both watched the road, like two people intent on a game, their team about to lose, no one breathing.

I put my hand on her, but gently, trying to tell her everything would be all right.

Chad called for me to hit her. "Go ahead and hit her," he was saying, his voice loud, from somewhere deep inside his body.

Even when a freeway overpass flashed over us, and then the road spread out, darkness everywhere, Raymond still had trouble with the car. By then it was plain to me that Raymond *wanted* to run into something—he hoped to slam into the timbers with their pretty red reflector lights along the road.

We half spun to avoid a sports car puttering along.

Raymond fought the wheel, getting the car back into control as we passed a long, low white building, Costco, with its broad, empty parking lot, and rows of shopping carts gleaming, chained together.

A pay phone glittered beside the planter-box of black plants. I had a flash thought, one of us spilling out of the car, sprinting for the phone.

The woman was not making a sound, folded over, trying to catch her breath, or getting ready to make a run.

Two radio transmitters loomed up into the night sky, red points of light strobing off and on at their twin summits. Raymond swung the car wide around the corner, tires squealing. Red reflectors indicated the end of the road, dark timber barriers suddenly white in the illumination from the headlights.

Chad uttered further instructions, words I could not catch. Raymond gunned the engine, and the Firebird lunged up over the curb, not with a rush—unevenly, lurching into the dark.

The ground here was rugged, the car bouncing, our heads hitting the ceiling. Great jagged brown boulders reflected the headlight beams, and Raymond stood on the brakes.

Chad flung open his door and was out of the car, yanking at the door beside me, the entire car rocking with his effort.

I levered the door handle, then thumbed the latch, unlocking the door and causing it to open so easily Chad was sent off balance, staggering backward.

He recovered his footing and leaned forward, his breath smelling of rum. "Bring her out," he said.

I was like someone who has run miles, a sour taste in my mouth. Raymond was backing away, a shape dancing back toward the lights of town and muted freeway glow, and when I called out to him he didn't say a word. He stopped and watched, too far off for his features to be clear.

I helped the woman out of the car, trying to keep my body between her and Chad, but she fought me. I shoved her along at arm's length, trying to give her the idea that this was when she should make her break, *get out of here.*

Raymond was gone, running back toward the town lights, and I tried to send him a psychic snapshot, the phone by the side of the road.

Chad brushed me aside, took her by one arm, and flung her

out, into the dry grass. She almost fell down. She was a pale, windswept smudge, struggling for footing in the oat weeds.

She put out her hands, like a person keeping a weight from falling in. Chad shot her.

CHAPTER TWENTY-NINE

"Why did you do that?"

Was it my voice asking the question?

It had to be, there was no one else.

Chad made some adjustment to the automatic, setting the safety, and then he stuck the gun under his shirt, having trouble, the pistol not fitting where he wanted it to go.

He said, "She saw our faces."

I moved past him, quickly, so I was between Chad and the woman lying on the ground.

He emptied the contents of the purse haphazardly, over the weeds in the headlight glare. Kleenex and breath mints, lipstick, half-lens reading glasses, with a strand of glass beads attached. Pocket calculator, a brace of colored pencils held together by a twisted rubber band.

Chad said, "She didn't have any money."

Chad took the eel-skin purse in both hands and pulled. He tore it in two, the last pennies and grocery lists tumbling, the cold air perfumed with tired peppermint. He found a side pocket in the purse, and forced a zipper. A red leather wallet tumbled out, and he knelt and unfastened the snap.

He straightened. "Seventeen dollars," he said, letting the wallet fall.

Chad peered back into the car, his head and shoulders full of color in the interior light, his skin flushed, his padded jacket sea blue. He looked over at me as though trying to remember who I was.

Compress the wound.

I took off my sweatshirt and folded it into a tight pack, and pressed down on the streaming bullet hole. I was sure I was too late, sure she was gone, but I felt for the pulse points in her neck. Her heart was beating. Her eyelids fluttered. I told her everything would be all right, forcing my voice to make a sound.

After a long stillness Chad pounded the top of the car with his fist. He pounded several times, hard, the metal buckling.

He wrestled the pistol out of his belt, and I heard the hard, sharp click of the weapon as he released the safety. He walked toward me, holding the gun down in both fists, straight-armed. He steadied himself and pointed the gun at her head.

I stood.

I didn't have time to set my feet.

I threw a straight right, a punch that whipped his skull back but didn't make him drop the gun. I hit him again, stepping right into it, backing him up. I felt something break in the front of his skull, a bone or a tooth.

I hit him again, hard, a left hook and a right cross.

He went down and didn't move.

* * *

The thrum and glitter of highway traffic was far away.

I knelt beside her. Her heart was still beating.

Her eyes were on mine. We both heard it, at first too distant to have anything to do with us, and then getting closer, the high-low tune of a siren.